PARLAY

PARLAY

M. J. Manley

VANTAGE PRESS
New York

Published by Vantage Press, Inc.
516 West 34th Street, New York, New York 10001

Manufactured in the United States of America
ISBN: 0-533-11863-8

Library of Congress Catalog Card No.: 96-90050

0 9 8 7 6 5 4 3 2 1

To all the mothers
who try so hard to give their children
a better life and make them better citizens,
which will make it a better world
for all of us

PARLAY

1

"All that glitters is not gold, at least that's the way it always has been, and always will be in my family, girl," said Paula in despair to her new-found friend, who just moved into the housing projects in North Las Vegas. "Girl, when I first moved to Las Vegas from Hollywood, California, there were all those bright lights and people standing at the front of those casinos just a-smilin' and tryin' to get me to come in and take my chances on that slot machine, the one in front of the Silver Slipper Casino.

"Why, I couldn't play that slot machine! I was holding Harold, my two-year-old son, on my right hip, and Sylvia, my baby, was in the stroller. Alongside me were two suitcases of luggage, along with those Pampers. But that slot machine was tempting. I had just got off at the Greyhound bus station that day in May and I was looking for the children's Uncle Harry. All I could hear was those bells, girl, and those thin pans just a-ringin' and that money droppin'. I thought that this was sure enough the place for me, the Land of Opportunity and Gold.

"That was over fifteen years ago, honey, and look where I am now—in this roach-infected, drug-dealing, back-stabbing housing project. And I'll be here until the day I die. If I'm lucky, those grown children of mine will have enough sense to get out of here and find a life for themselves out of Las Vegas. But I ain't lucky, girl. If I were, I wouldn't be here in this stinking housing project,

1

in this greedy and corrupt town, Las Vegas. If I was lucky, I would be dead and taken away from all this misery. I would rather be dead."

Paula Simmons and her two children had come to Las Vegas, Nevada, more than fifteen years ago, looking for a new way of life and a way to raise her children in the American dream—yeah, that classic American way of living in a house and walking your children to the school bus stop without fearing those children would be brutally murdered or propositioned by drug dealers and child molesters. In Hollywood, she had hoped one day to be an actress, a star.

"Girl," Paula angrily raised her voice, addressing her new young neighbor, "the only stars I saw were those stars on the bus while I was en route to the hellhole. I couldn't let the children see me crying; I had to be strong, girl. I had to show them that you have to be strong in this world, you can't give up, you got to have faith. From the time those kids were babies I tried to show them how to survive and not depend on other people, black or white. Besides, all the people here in North Las Vegas are just good-for-nothing Negroes."

The young girl jumped out of her chair, not to avoid the cockroaches, but startled at Paula's tone of voice and her theatrical mannerism as she tried to explain to the new girl in the housing projects how things really were in Las Vegas.

"Negroes come in all colors and varieties, girl, not just black. They are white, brown, all nationalities. And, girl, when you mix them up with that green stuff—yes, money—you get the same color out of all of them. Purple. Yes, girl, the color purple. I mean to tell you, sweetie, this place ain't no Alice Walker novel. This place stinks with contempt and greed, with people trying to get over on you, using any means necessary. Honey, this place is a melting pot for con artists and hustlers. It's their world. Those shysters and high-rollers, why, they'd put their own mothers on the corner for just a few nickels more. And the women who live here, girl, they'll stab you in the back so fast you won't even know you're bleeding!"

"Well, Ms. Simmons," said the young girl nervously, "thank you for the orientation, but I've got to go back to my apartment. I think I hear the baby crying." She was anxious to leave Paula's small, one-bedroom, smoke-filled apartment.

"Take my advice, honey. The fewer people you deal with in Las Vegas, the better off you'll be. And one other thing, don't let me scare you, sweetie. Maybe you'll be able to adjust here. That's just my personal point of view on this hellhole. But you're young and you got that baby to raise. Things are a little bit different now, I guess. This is 1996, and maybe you can find a job and a good man to help raise that son of yours. If you need anything, just come on over, honey. Come on and talk to Granny. That's what they call me now, Granny, because I know the ins and outs of the city. I guess I'm an old pro now at this vicious cycle of life."

Poor child, thought Paula, just eighteen years old and with a child already. These "chillen" should think about those kids that they're bringing into this world. I'm not one who believes in abortion, because I love my children, but the world and this society are going to abort those kids down the road anyway, with all those drugs and discrimination. Why, you got to be a saint in order to get a good job these days. I'm willing to give anybody good odds that if Jesus Christ, our Savior, came back today from Heaven even He would be discriminated against. Things are worse now than they ever were!

Speaking of babies, I better check on my grandbaby. She'd been asleep for a long time. That mother of hers still hadn't got back home yet. Why, Sylvia had been gone all night. Seventeen years old and out on the streets until the early morning; she was probably using those damn drugs again.

Paula thought to herself, When I raised her up, I would never have thought I'd see her abusing drugs, let alone going around prostituting her body just to get some more of that crack cocaine. It ain't nothing but evil out there on those streets, and that brother of hers is probably the one who is selling her the drugs. Does Harold think I can't see him from her kitchen window, out on the street right in front of the housing project, selling crack cocaine to every car that passes by!

What was a mother to do? She'd thrown him out of the house several times, and he'd promised not to ever sell drugs again. But there weren't no jobs for these young people, and they all had their needs and wants.

As Granny Paula looked out the kitchen window she could see her son on the corner, wearing a skullcap, a jacket three times his size, and overalls that resembled the Farmer Johns that Mr. Green Jeans used to wear. That boy was down there again selling those drugs right in front of the projects. Why, if the social worker came by here this morning and saw him out there, we would all be evicted. All he thought about was his damn selfish ass, just like his father—conceited and self-centered. She was willing to bet that he'd come home complaining that he hadn't got no money, and here she was looking at him selling those damned drugs right there in broad daylight.

He'd better have some money to give her. She'd lost all of her money on that damned slot machine and wouldn't get her county check until next week. That boy better have some money for her for some food. Why, he was twenty years old now and had more criminal convictions than Todd Bridges, that childhood actor she'd done a few scenes with years ago as an amateur actress in Hollywood. That son of hers would probably tell her he hadn't got one red penny. That dope-dealing little hustler was just like his lazy-ass father, just like him, Paula thought to herself as she continued to look out the window.

Harold was heading toward the apartment now, after selling drugs all night out there in the streets, trudging home to get some sleep, like he'd been working the graveyard shift bringing in time and a half on his paycheck. Yeah, he'd get time and a half when they picked him up for dealing drugs, the big overgrown fool. He was already on probation, and the next time he went to jail they'd give him five years. She was willing to bet that he'd go straight when he got out of that prison, with all of those homosexuals and homicidal prisoners.

She'd done everything she could for that boy, but he was just like his father—stubborn and foolish. Why couldn't a good-looking boy like him find a nice girlfriend and settle down? But no, he thought he was too good for nice girls, and those girls on the street spoiled him, giving him sex and money whenever he whispered in their little ears. He'd lost all respect for women, or at least those kinds of women—those "Strawberry Girls" who wanted cocaine from him and would do anything for him to get it.

One day when she was walking home from the grocery store she'd seen her son and Esther Lee, a girl who lived a few doors down, in the alley having oral sex. She'd called to Harold, but he'd still kept at it, holding that young girl's head down between his long legs and going at it; he didn't budge and neither did she. Those drugs did something to those women. It was scary and frightening.

She was willing to lay odds that his sister was out there doing the same things to men just to get drugs, turning tricks for those drugs!

"Mom, I'm home," Harold said as he entered the one-bedroom tenement apartment as if he'd been working all night on a blue-collar job. "Is there anything cooked for breakfast?" She slapped him hard. "What the hell did you slap me for? What did I do this time?"

"You know what the hell you did. You were out there dealing those drugs again, you little bastard."

"Well, you're nothing but a bitch," Harold responded. He was shocked to discover that his mother had been watching him through the kitchen window at an angle as he dealt drugs right down the street from the housing tenements. "My mouth is bleeding! Look what you did! You made my mouth bleed!"

"Didn't I tell you not to be dealing those drugs?"

"Yeah, you told me, just like you told me a lot of things. Like those fairy tales about how I'd grow up and be a doctor or an attorney. That we live in a free society, and that all men and women are equal. Yeah, you told me a lot of fuckin' bullshit when I was younger, just like you told me not to deal drugs. But I like nice things in life, just like the white people. But the white man controls every goddamn thing, so what you told me about getting a good education and going to college didn't mean a damned thing in their racist-ass America. This is a double-standard system where they control the jobs, they control the resources, and they control the distribution of all the wealth.

As Black people, we don't control a damned thing but the corners of our block, where we push drugs and sell them to our own people. We sell poison to our own people, Mama, and who do you think we get those kilos of drugs from? The white man sells us the drugs. So don't tell me a damned thing about me making a little money to buy that dick-sucking sister of mine's baby some Pampers.

"And don't you tell me a damned thing about the money I give you, when you run right downtown and put all your money into those damn slots. I was just trying to help you, Mama, and help the family, and dealing drugs all night on that corner is the only means possible. I'm getting out of here. You're not gonna slap me around no more."

"Son, don't leave us. I'm sorry for slapping you, but you know how I feel about those drugs."

"Know how you feel? What the hell do you mean? You're nothing but a junkie yourself, a slot-machine junkie. You're no better than those bitches who go around selling their bodies and souls just for a hit of the drug I sell them. You're on the gambling drug, an addicted gambler, just like I'm addicted to drug dealing because I want something out of life, 'money,' and just like Sylvia, your daughter, is addicted to crack cocaine. So don't give me no shit about you wanting me to stop dealing drugs. You stop gambling your county check away, you stop gambling away Dad's pension check, and I'll stop dealing drugs."

"Son, please don't leave us! I'll stop betting on those horses and stop playing the slot machines all night if you'll just stay here. You're the only one I can trust. If you leave, those gang bangers will kill us; they'll rob us. You protect us, son, so please don't leave us.

"No, Mom, not this time. I'm going to Uncle Harry's to live. I'm sick and tired of you and Sis always putting me down and trying to control me when you two got worse problems. She's a cocaine addict, Mom, a compulsive drug addict. Every time you mention drugs she starts to shake and go take a shit. She's gone, Mom.

7

"And that little crackhead baby of hers. Who's the daddy? She got that baby pulling a trick for some drugs. That baby is retarded, Mom, high on those drugs that Sylvia uses.

"And look at you. Every time you hear those slot machine Looney Tunes and that clinking of the money hitting those tin trays, you get the shakes. You'd put every red cent in that slot machine, just like Sylvia would suck any and every man's dick in this housing apartment complex just for drugs. Yeah, look at it, right here in my hand. Rock cocaine. It's my way out of this junkie jungle."

"You're going to regret it, son," Paula yelled out to Harold as he stepped fast out of the housing project. "Your Uncle Harry is nothing but a crossroader, a con artist and a high-roller, and when the mob comes to kill him, they'll get you, too. He'll set you up, son. He's just like your daddy, a good-for-nothing hustler, and he'll only hammer the nails in your coffin."

The yelling and arguing brought all the neighbors out of the housing project as Harold left in a frantic hurry.

"What's wrong, Mrs. Simmons? Did you have another argument with your son?" the young next-door neighbor asked. "You might as well just let that fool go. He'll have to learn the hard way, just like the rest of them. Learn right before they kill them. They're all no good, honey."

"I tried my best to do what I could for that boy, even sent him to junior college, but still he winds up dealing drugs on the street."

"Well, he's going to miss the baby," the neighbor said.

"Oh, sure. He never cared for his little niece. Just this morning he called her a crack-head baby!"

"No, Mrs. Simmons, I mean his baby. Yes, your grandson. I had Harold's baby, but we were afraid to tell you that the baby was his until things got better. I wanted to wait until Harold got a job and got away from all the drug dealing and hustling before we told you, Mrs. Simmons. I love Harold, but I couldn't keep it a secret any longer. You gained a grandson, Mrs. Simmons, and you lost a son!"

Paula Simmons sat down in shock and dismay. "I always thought that Harold was gay because I never saw him with a girl, unless that girl was paying him off sexually for a drug debt."

"I know, Mrs. Simmons, but I was willing to accept that in Harold, those strange ways of his and his infrequent social behavior, because I love him. Now I have some of him in the baby."

"Well, sister, join the club of idiots," Paula Simmons said. "You'll fit in with the rest of us nuts very well. You sure had me fooled!" They hugged each other and wiped away their tears as Mrs. Simmons looked at her newly discovered two-week-old grandson with surprise and dismay.

*　　*　　*

North Las Vegas is an area in Las Vegas set aside for poor and low-income people. The city council's plans were to keep them in their place by devising a borderline across the railroad tracks, as if the people were animals, allowed to live in one specific area, but unable to leave that certain defined area, with the railroad tracks acting as a barbed-wire fence so the low-income people would not go astray. It proved worthy. During the 1965 Watts riots and the most recent 1992 Los Angeles riots, Las Vegas had felt a ripple effect, with looters breaking into expensive furniture stores and taking durable items such as refrigerators and couches, only to be arrested, since those items were too heavy and too complicated to carry back

9

across the railroad tracks to the junkie jungle in the housing projects.

Paula heard the front door open and softly close. "Sylvia, is that you? Where have you been all night and day?"

"I've been out looking for a job," Sylvia said.

"A job? What kind of job?" Mrs. Simmons wiped the corner of her mouth where saliva had run down, indicating that she'd been in a deep and serious sleep. "What kind of job have you been looking for, gone two days and leaving me with this baby."

"Mama, I walked all the way downtown and I went to every casino, inquiring about a position as a cocktail waitress. I got my sheriff's card from the police station, and I must have filled out thirteen applications, starting at the Union Plaza Hotel and ending up all the way at the other end at the El Cortez Hotel and Casino."

"You lying bitch, you been on those drugs again, haven't you?"

"No, Mama, I've been looking for a job."

"You must think I was born yesterday! Look at your hair and those clothes. You've been lying down on your back pulling tricks for those drugs. Don't lie to me, heifer. Why, you got to be twenty-one just to get a sheriff's card. Do you think I'm stupid? You smell terrible. You must have been in one of those crack houses smoking that cocaine all night. Get right in there and take a bath right this minute, Sylvia."

Sylvia tried to slip past her mother on her way to the bathroom, only to catch a right fist in the back of the head that knocked her into the wall. "Mama, don't hit me no more. I'm sorry. It won't happen again."

"That's what your brother said, and he now done left out of here to go live with your Uncle."

10

"Harold's gone?"

"Yes, Harold moved away. Now it's just you, me, and that crack-head baby of yours. Oh, by the way, Harold has given us a new addition. Barbara, the new girl who lives a few doors down, is claiming that the two-week-old baby of hers is your brother's. So one is gone, and one is here to raise. What's the difference? Harold had the mind of a two-year-old baby anyway, always hustling those drugs."

"My brother is gone! Oh no, now what are we going to do, Mama? How am I going to feed my baby and buy Pampers? That's why I went to go find a job. I knew something like this was going to happen," she wailed.

"You never missed Harold before. And the both of you used to fight like cats and dogs. It's those drugs you used to steal from Harold, that's your real concern, ain't it? Harold used to tell me that he lost some money right here while he was sleeping on that couch. You were stealing from Harold, weren't you, girl? You even smoked all of those little cocaine candies he had in that little plastic bag of his."

Sylvia hissed at her mother, "You loved Harold more, and never gave a damn about me. You bought Harold everything, and left me raggedy. Well, I wanted some nice things, too. I wanted to look nice with some new shoes and a dress when I was going to school, but you used all of Dad's pension money on those slots. That money was supposed to be used for us. We were supposed to get an allotment, but you played "Lots of Slots" at the Silver Slipper Casino every time the mailman dropped that check inside that mailbox. That was our money. Dad died for us, serving his country, and you just threw that money away each and every month. That's why we're here, living in this junkie jungle. You're nothing but a junkie, Mama, a slot machine junkie."

Most Las Vegas welfare recipients, Social Security recipients, and military retirement pensioners got their checks on the first and third of every month, only to spend every red cent on a bus tour to Las Vegas, Nevada. The hotels and casinos knew this, so they beefed up the advertisements and tightened the slot machines on the first and third days of each month, knowing on the fifth day and the remaining days of each month, the same people who worked inside the casinos would spend their last dollar of wages and tips during the remaining days of the month, gambling and wishing and praying that their number, their magic number, would come up.

But statistics proved that 90% percent of the time the million-dollar pay-offs were won by some outsider from some small city who was just passing through. This strategy of baiting the fish paid the light bills and made a handsome eight billion dollars full profit per year in Las Vegas.

* * *

Paula Simmons's life was at a crossroads. Harold was a drug dealer, peddling small pieces of poison. His sister, Sylvia, was his best customer—a drug user and a street whore. Maybe she should have stayed in Hollywood, California. Moving here to Las Vegas was the biggest mistake of her life. All she wanted to do was to raise her two kids in a nice environment and give them an opportunity at life, something she'd never had. But now she'd come to realize that life was an equal opportunity struggle, and everybody must die. Before death there was a constant struggle for survival, with some people finding heaven on earth and others living in a constant hell.

The dream was right in front of her eyes—all that money out there, the flashy lights, the rich fancy cars, the beautiful homes. But all she got to do was clean up the mess those rich white people made, scrubbing their floors and making up their beds after they screwed everything that came through their front doors during exotic nights of partying and orgies. Well, at least when Mrs. Elderman came and picked her up to do some cleaning for her, she paid well. She even got to bring home some of the leftovers from those parties. Thank God she was still able to work a little.

Just think, these kids' father had served over twenty years in the military, fighting during three conflicts in which the United States government was involved, and the only thing they had to show for it was a one-bedroom tenement apartment full of cockroaches and rats.

Why, if Harold Sr. were alive today, they would be living in Beverly Hills. He was a skirt chaser, but in a crisis he did provide for his family. His family always came first. Maybe that's why Harold Junior was the way he was. Lord have mercy, he did try to look out for us, and he did risk his life out there dealing drugs on those corners all night to bring in a little extra cash so they could eat. She hadn't thought of it that way. She wished she hadn't slapped him.

2

"Son, you got to get it while you're young," Uncle Harry was telling Harold. "Why, when I was your age I always had a pocketful of money and a girl on my left arm and a girl on my right arm. Your dad and I were the talk of the town when we were growing up in Atlanta, Georgia. I taught your dad everything he knew, just like I'll teach you. You'll never have to deal drugs again, and your mom will be real proud of you. But you must pay close attention to what I am telling you, son, very close attention, because one little slip-up will cost you your life."

"My life, Uncle Harry? You don't plan on robbing a bank, do you?"

"Oh no, son, robbing banks was in my younger days. It's 1996, and I'm no spring chicken. Everything is done by computers now. This is the age of technology, and right here in Las Vegas is where all of the money is being transferred and transacted around you, over your head and even through your legs."

"Why, son, you're living in a fool's paradise right here in Las Vegas, Nevada; the fools come in, lose their damn life savings and laugh about losing with every pull of the slot machine, while those corporate owners design casinos to look like paradise, and you died and went to heaven when you have really gone to hell," Harry acclaimed, as if he was one of the chosen few from a higher source to convince the people in the city of sin to repent.

"So why do they do it, Uncle Harry? Why do people come here from all over the world just to feel happy for a few seconds and then sad when they lost all their money?" Harold said in a low-pitched voice with eyes of total curiosity as to why people spent over 330 billion dollars a year in gambling worldwide.

"It's all mass trickery, son; why, I can still remember when you and your sister were growing up, me and your mom took you and your cousins to Disneyland—just to see your eyes and the smiles on your faces when we were finally on our way to Los Angeles to Disneyland and how heartbroken you were when that five-second ride on the Mattehorn was over and you kept looking for more, more of a thrill, a maximum high like that first ride on the Mattehorn at Disneyland, but you never got it, you never reached that threshold again. Although you rode on that ride until the fantasy park closed and then you had to face reality, back to the bottom, North Las Vegas. You were fooled, son; you were tricked like all the other people that come to Las Vegas and see the money and the glamour—they, too, reach their maximum high, they, too, get a sensation of freedom and power surrounded by all that money and controlling the actions on the slot machine and those dice tables, but they too got to come back to reality, dead broke, but with that sensation of reaching that threshold again—they come back in the millions and some never leave trying to reach their peak," Harry explained as if he too were one of the millions that got hooked on the drug called fantasy and then had to face reality, broke and powerless.

Harold began to laugh and for the first time in his life he felt there was a little ray of hope, having been taught something about life from his father's brother. Harold never had a chance to be with his father much, and when he died, he'd had to take on the insurmountable responsibility of looking after his mom and sister while growing up in the junkie jungle of North Las Vegas.

"We'll start from scratch, and I'll show you how to parlay your talents."

"Parlay, parlay? What is a parlay, Uncle Harry?"

"Well, son, it's a little too early in the game right now to give you the whole strategy of what is and isn't a parlay, but I will define the word. A parlay is an equal, a pair, a bet, an original wager plus its winnings on a race, contest or whatever in life that it pertains to. In other words, it's the exploitation of someone who has it all. It is money or intelligence and taking that talent, intelligence, or finance to better oneself.

"You see, son, life is nothing but a big gamble, and you go through life betting on this, wanting and betting on that, needing and betting on good health, rather than at the race track or at the church testifying. You must survive and you must take chances in life. Life is nothing but a parlay of little bets, and the more things in life that you bet on, the better are your chances of success."

"Are people that sick, I mean, is that drug that potent Uncle, that people would lose everything in their life just to get back to a fantasy world and dream?"

"Yes, son, and the casino owners know what drives them in by the millions while they drive out penniless—it's subliminal son, they use that research passed down by those psychologists on how the brain works; that's why there are no clocks inside the casino so people won't have no sense of time, and all the drinks are free to make people feel loose and important—time is no problem, they say to themself and that's when they start thinking that money is no problem either."

As Harold listened to his Uncle Harry he thought

about his mother and how she was tricked all of those years to thinking that she could win; win enough to buy some extra food for him and his sister who were struggling to survive in the projects in North Las Vegas; win enough money to buy Harold and his sister Sylvia some clothes at Kmart instead of waiting in those long lines at St. Vincent homeless shelters for the give-aways. Harold thought back to how his mother was fooled subliminally, the word that his Uncle Harry used, to think that if she won enough money she would take him and his sister out of the City of Sin, but it never happened; she never won.

"What's wrong, son? Why, you look as if you seen a ghost," said Harry, now looking at Harold. The expression on his face was the same as the day that they all went to Disneyland, a place where dreams can come true with just one maximum peak experience and then the real world of reality grabs you like it just grabbed Harold.

"My mother, those bastards used that subliminal shit on my mother! They brainwashed her, Uncle Harry; she's a slot machine junkie and they are the dealers."

"Now you know what I mean, son; you see the light— why, it took me more than thirty years to figure it out, and it only took you thirty seconds." Harry, now placing his right hand on the shoulder of Harold, gave Harold a firm but gentle squeeze of confidence as Harry smiled in a gesture of saying to his nineteen-year-old nephew, "Welcome to the team, son."

Harry Simmons was from the old gentry of Atlanta, Georgia, where he was known as Big Daddy to all the young fillies and ladies of the evening. The menfolks called him the Black Colonel Sanders, after the fried-chicken millionaire, since Uncle Harry was a debonair-looking gentlemen with striking good looks and fine features. He had salt-and-pepper hair with a barber's bar moustache, and he had a habit of always twisting his moustache at the ends while trying to get his point across to his assailants and friends. Although his great-grandfathers had been slaves in the deep South of Atlanta, Georgia, Uncle Harry was a Confederate and took on all the ways of his former people's former masters. As Uncle Harry would jokingly tell folks, he was a direct descendent of Thomas Jefferson, but his conception was consummated behind the hen house, not in the parlor. Still he kept those humble and cheerful jaunty characteristics from the good old school of the South.

Eighteen hundred miles away in Las Vegas, Nevada, Uncle Harry was well known as a crossroader, or a con artist in simpler terms. Uncle Harry was a better crossroader than a ladies' man in Las Vegas. He would cheat a bum holding up a cardboard sign saying: "Will Work For Food" out of his take for that day and his sign, just for the challenge and to find out how gullible a person could possibly be.

In Harry's younger days in Las Vegas he would use a small drill bit and a battery-powered drill to stick a fine wire through the glass and hold all three cherries on the slot machine to win the jackpot. Harry was the King of the Crossroaders, before those electronic gadgets and surveillance cameras were installed at all the casinos, in the good old days of gambling in Las Vegas. Then the King of Crossroading was sent out to pasture, when those new computer chip circuits took over Vegas and all his hustling days were through.

But Harry was smart. He still believed in the old French Quarter's game of parlaying one's life. So he enrolled at the University of Nevada, Las Vegas, learning all about sophisticated surveillance camera techniques and computer equipment and asking every question conceivable to the professors and the technicians of the technical communications department to learn about electronic transfer of funds by computer. He studied how those computer chips that were installed in the new slot machines were used to pay off Mega-Buck Millions when all the sevens, and cherries, and the bars lined up precisely and to the wire, that is, that electronic chip wire. Uncle Harry had a plan.

*　　*　　*

"Sylvia," Paula yelled out to the living room. "Sylvia, turn down that music, honey. Me and the baby are trying to sleep. Have a little consideration. Why, you could wake up the dead with all that loud rap music!"

"It's not rap music, Mama, it's Prince and the Revolution, and he's singing your song."

"What? What song are you talking about? Are you trying to get smart with me again?"

"No, Mama, just listen to the song called '7' that I borrowed from Barbara," Sylvia said placing the tape inside the tape player.

"Why, you little smart-ass bitch, you knew I stopped gambling the day you stopped sneaking outside at night, going down to the crack house to get yourself some of that rock cocaine. Now what the hell are you insinuating?"

"Mama, I could always talk to you before, but now you're trying to ignore me. I'm going through some withdrawal and I need some money for treatment."

"Treatment, what kind of treatment? The last time you had treatment at the county hospital, you ran off with their television set and sold the TV and the treatment tape to one of your junkie friends. Luckily, you were a minor or you'd still be locked up in juvenile hall. Now what are you saying, girl?"

"Well, I get chills down my spine and get hyped up, just like you do, Mama, around the first of the month, when you keep on pacing the floor and looking out the window for that mailman to arrive with your welfare check and Dad's pension check. You can't wait to get that check so you can go lose it all on those slot machines, can you? Well, I'm giving you some of your own medicine. We'll both be sitting here going through cold turkey withdrawals. We made a pledge together, Mama, and now the both of us will withdraw from our addiction, whether it's the slots or the rock."

"Sylvia honey, I don't know about you, but the first of the month is Friday, and those checks will be hitting the box in a few days. I've been sitting here all month with you, taking care of your baby, and now I want to go out and get a breath of fresh air. I can't wait to get to the casino again."

"You'll be waiting a long time, Mama."

"What?" Paula said.

"I wrote a letter to the Department of Veteran Affairs and told them that you've never given Harold or me one red cent of Dad's money, so they're going to hold your benefits pending further investigation. They'll be calling Harold over at Uncle Harry's house, also."

"Oh, no! You didn't, child. That money is to put a roof over our heads. That money is to buy food for me, you and the baby. I know you didn't write them and tell them that I wasn't giving you your portion. Please tell me that you didn't write them, Sylvia."

"I did, Mama. It's the best way to kick your habit of compulsive gambling."

"Why, you stupid little bitch! I'm going to kick your lit-

20

tle ass!" The fighting commenced, and Paula whipped Sylvia real good. Sylvia yelled back, but never hit her mom.

"You never put a roof over our heads, Mama. We're here on Section 8 and the government pays our rent. You never feed us, you get food stamps. So don't give me that shit about what you did for us, 'cause you never did a mother-fucking thing for us but leave us in this raggedy-ass housing project alone every first of the month while you put on those cheap shoes of yours and that raggedy sweater and went out there with all your lovers. Yes, your lovers—those slot machines you been romancing. Those slot machines took our money, Mama, the money that Dad set up for us. We never received one red cent!"

It came with the territory once you were on the turf of the casinos. Although Paula and Sylvia were having problems communicating with each other the two had the same dysfunctional characteristic. Paula, once fascinated with the bright lights and the constant flow of money when she first entered Las Vegas, Nevada, from Hollywood, experienced something that she never experienced before in her life, opportunity. It surrounded her, the freedom to display her talents and have another chance at life, that chance to make it as a show dancer and maybe someday become a choreographer.

"You're just a damn liar, just like your daddy was, talking all out of your head, girl—it's those damn drugs, that rock cocaine in your system—it done burned out the little sense you once had," Paula yelled out, loud enough she could not hear Sylvia and the truth; the truth about all the years of her receiving government money and never spending that money to better herself and her children, just making it better for the casino owners as profits sky-rocketed.

21

"If I'm a liar why are we still here in this roach den, Momma, and look at you, you're a mess, your hair ain't combed and your face ain't washed, but by the first of the month you'll fix yourself up real pretty, with lipstick and that mop, that you call hair, will be all pressed and you'll be ready for your date once that check get here, your date with Mr. Lots Of Slots, that little machine that's been pimping you all these years and putting you on your back. Not at some sleeze whorehouse but right here, on your back, broke, right here in the North Las Vegas Housing Projects."

"At least I'm not on my back all night fucking every man that rolls down main street just for a drag of that rock cocaine—just look at yourself, child, you look as old as me. And those legs of yours is just as a-skinny as the legs on that kitchen table—what with you, what does that shit do to you anyway; you were a beautiful child and now you're just a-skitter selling your body for a drag off a crack pipe," Paula said, as the two looked each other up and down like two boxers entering the ring before the bell, picking at each other to find out what would set the other one off so badly that punches would be thrown between the two.

"I make more money lying on my back than you do standing straight up, jacking off on those slot machine handles all night, Momma."

"Well, where is the money; every time you come through that damn door you smellin' like a skunk and looking like a possum, with your hair all sticking out from your head like you put your hand through an electric socket; where is the money you get from lying on your back all night for those five dollar tricks?"

"The same place where your money is—the dope man got it. But your dope man is a machine and you feed

22

him all night long, just a-putting those coins into him, and he telling you to play me more; well, the dope man around the corner where I spent my money has a slot on his iron gate, too, Momma, and he says "Pay Me More," he don't accept credit just like that little dope man of yours at the casino, and he just a-laugh, slam that iron gate in my face when I ask him please, just like that little Looney Tune slot machine that you play with all night and all day until you're broke and come walking home with that cigarette-smoked sweater all hanging off you, walking with your head looking down on the ground to see if you can find some money that someone dropped so you can play with the little dope man again, Momma," Sylvia screamed as she ran to the small bathroom crying after giving her mother a little piece of her mind.

"Oh Lord, what have I done to these children—they been watching me all these years and ain't said a word to me—I'm the reason they ain't no good, it's because of me, it's my fault, we are all the same."

Laughing and crying together, both of them embraced, held each other and realized that their whole family was breaking up because of their compulsiveness, whether it was drugs or gambling. Things had to change in their lives before someone ended up dead or in a state of no return.

"We got to change, Sylvia. You're right. We must change our lives. I'm glad you did that, stopping my checks the way you did. I'm glad that you made me realize what a tyrant I've been, spending the money your Dad sacrificed his life for. Here we are, living in poverty, and I'm making excuses that the government deserted us and saying it's because of racism that we are stuck here in this poverty-stricken housing project. You're right, honey. We got to get back on our feet and do something for ourselves

or this whole welfare system and gambling will be rein-
acted with our grandkids."

"Yes, Mama, this is the only way for us to realize our
faults, and that's to look at it from another point of view.
We became too dependent on our welfare checks."

"You're right, oh wise daughter, and that's why I
called the county on you and told them you were using
drugs. I was so afraid you'd sneak out of the house when
you got your check and start using those drugs again.
Why, your heart could have gone out, or you could have
ended up dead from those gang member drug dealers that
you owe all that money to. And now that Harold's gone,
there's no one here to protect us."

"You did what?" Sylvia shrieked. "I know damn well
you didn't stop my county check, Mama."

"Yes, I did. Here, let me show you the letter they sent
you. Here it is. It states that all of your benefits will be cancelled immediately."

"You read my mail and cancelled my check! Why, you
dirty-ass conniving bitch!"

"Don't you talk to your mother that way! Besides,
President Clinton is reforming the welfare system, and you
would have been cut off the system anyway with the new
training program he's initiating. Now you have a jump on
everybody. At least you're still alive, and pretty soon
you'll be drug free, honey!"

"Okay, Mama, if you can do it, so can I. Let's call
Uncle Harry and ask him if we can move in with him and
Harold and start a new life."

"Okay, sweetheart. It's worth a try."

*   *   *

From previous treatment at the Compulse behavior

center they both knew that compulsive behavior cannot be seen unless a person steps out of the environment in which that compulsion is being exhibited; it is like seeing yourself on television and noticing that your hair isn't combed right or the lipstick you're wearing is too red and thick in one place or is too bright. "It looks like I am too dark (or light) on that video," one might say. "Was the color adjusted on the camera?"

Compulsive behavior can be excessive spending at the mall or using one's credit card too often. Everybody has a different compulsive behavior and gratification, whether it be sports or drugs, gambling, or even the desire to commit murder.

Compulsion is defined by the American Psychology Association as a psychological state in which an individual acts against his own will or conscious inclinations, and compulsion forces an individual to act against his own wishes.

Las Vegas has all the ingredients for an individual to act against his own free will. The lights in the casinos stimulate the retina in the eye and act as a mechanism that keeps a person wide awake and energetic, while the sounds used on the slot machines stimulate the hypo-thalamus and its sensory organs; a sound of delight, a sound that says, "Play me; don't worry, you will win on the next turn."

But that turn never comes. The sounds that are used to lure people into the casinos are embedded in our minds, stemming perhaps all the way back to a nursery rhyme song. Yes, those funny little sounds that your mother and dad used to play to get you to sleep when you were an infant. You'll hear those same sounds at the video arcade, and you'll hear the same sounds when you are dead broke after spending all of your money, thinking that the slot machine will pay off eventually.

Kids are being subjected to these sounds as early as infancy, and, with the Nintendo games, that compulsive sound will always be embedded in the memory of the mind. This is the main reason Las Vegas is turning its wheels 360 degrees and making it a kid's town for recreation. Big business is well aware that kids lure in parents, and parents bring money to the City of Sin. The water parks and the arcades are getting larger, while peoples' minds are getting more narrow and compulsive.

It's a psychological game of latent memories and conditioning. And you can't win.

3

"No, Uncle Harry, tell them no. It's been a whole month since I left home, and I've been doing great here with you. And now Mom and Sylvia want to move in? Just tell them no, hell no!" Harold said.

"They're my niece and my brother's wife. I can't deny them a place to live. Besides, there's plenty of room here. We'll all be very comfortable here, one big family."

"Well, what're they going to do with that crackhead baby with the big head and large eyes? That baby cries all night. That baby is like his mother, up all night and sleeps all day. Crack cocaine is still in that crackhead kid's system, and you're going to have to get a major exorcism to get that baby's system clean," said Harold.

"Let's give them a week and see how it works out. Besides, we can use your sister and mom to help us with "Operation Parlay." If this operation goes according to plan, all of us will be wealthy!"

As Harry thought about how he would place his new parlay of players in his scheme, his mustache started to twitch.

"Harold, you're the finest nephew an uncle can have and what I like about you is that you listen—now when your sister and mother arrive we got to treat them right, I mean, I know how it was in the past. The fights that the three of you were engaged in was big enough to call in the National Guard, but those days are all over my son, you see, we got to prove to my sister-in-law and niece that the plan that I made will work, Son," Harry said, now walking in circles around Harold with one hand twisting his long Van Dyke mustache while the other hand folded over his beer belly, walking and talking, at the same time trying to convince Harold in an obscure manner that adding two more players to his parlay would not harm a thing, but it would take just a few dollars out of his pocketbook.

"Uncle Harry, why I am shocked at you; after all that you have told me about how the Big Bosses inside those casinos capture the people and make them, out of their own personal money, laundering puppets, you're planning on doing the same thing to your own niece and sister-in-law," Harold acclaimed, now making eye-to-eye contact with Uncle Harry, a technique that the old King of the Crossroaders taught his nephew and heir to his throne during the first week of his apprenticeship.

"Well, Son, I just thought that we could . . . "

"That's an excellent idea, Uncle; why not use them . . . why if my mother stayed in those dirty, filthy housing projects she'd be used and spit out, all worn out— going down to the county office every other day and haggling with those social workers, trying to beg them for more food stamps to feed me, Sylvia, and that little crack-head baby—use them, Uncle, and show them how to make a decent living by ripping people off."

"Why, Harold, I am appalled and very proud of you, you learn quick, Son, and I guess it's all contributed to the training I showed you on how those Big Bosses bait people inside their casinos by feeding them, giving them drinks and a nice inexpensive place to stay for the night, when in all actuality they are bound to spend ten times the amount by gambling their fool heads off," Harry said in a convincing and most confident manner, reassuring Harold that there would be no harm done to his sister and mother, and that they would benefit from his Operation Parlay with a "handsome" amount of revenue.

"You'll be able to give both of them enough money to make up for all the rip-offs that they been through from the casinos and the drug dealers, won't you, Uncle Harry?"

"Well, son, it's worth a try; the big payback comes in many forms and six dollar figures. Let us just pray that we land a big catch so the bread can be distributed fairly and all of us can have our palms of our hands squeezed gracefully with the legal 'tender'ly."

"Amen, Uncle Harry, amen. Do you want me to call them or do you want to pass on the good news to them?" Harold said. "But, Uncle Harry, don't say I didn't warn you. Why, Sylvia looks like a prune now since she's been smoking that crack cocaine. And Mom takes all her money and gambles it all as soon as the mailman delivers it." Harold tried emphatically to explain to his uncle his previous experiences with his mom and sister.

"Harold, they're all the family that either of us has now, and we got to take care and look after each other. Times are hard for all of us and we must parlay all of our skills."

"Parlay, parlay," said Harold. "You parlay with somebody that got money, but they ain't got a penny. Didn't they tell you that both of their checks were cut off? They probably snitched on each other, and the government cut both of their welfare checks off. They'll be totally dependent on us, just like last time. We're the ones who'll pay for their compulsive behaviors."

"Give it a few weeks, and let's see how it works out, Harold. Give it some time."

"Well, okay, Uncle Harry. Besides, this is your house, not mine."

"No, son, this is our house I purchased with the money your grandparents left us in their will after our land in Atlanta, Georgia, was sold. This house belongs to the family. Your mom and sister are coming over to live this afternoon, so let's get prepared for them."

*   *   *

The cab driver was shaking like a California earthquake, and he could have tilted the Richter scale over ten points as he hurried and loaded up the luggage inside the trunk of the cab.

"Let's hurry, ma'am, the meter is still running."

"It's not supposed to be running," Sylvia stated. "We haven't gone nowhere yet."

"Well, I got another call, lady, way on the other side of town, so let's hurry. And make sure that you have the correct change."

"Mister, all you want to know is if I have any money at all. But you can believe one thing—my brother-in-law, Harry Simmons, will have the money for you, he certainly will, when we get to his house," said Paula Simmons.

"Harry Simmons? You mean Big Daddy of the Good Old South? He's your brother-in-law?"

"Yes, he's my brother-in-law. Do you know him?" asked Paula.

"Do I know him? Why, when I first arrived here in Las Vegas I messed around at those casinos and was flat busted, and Harry helped me find shelter and food. I told him I'd pay him back one day, but he never would accept a penny from me. It'll be a pleasure for an old Irishman like me to escort you to the Simmons estate. Here, let me help you with the rest of your luggage."

"You see there, Sylvia? Already things are changing

in our lives for the better," Paula said.

"Yes, Mama, and we haven't even left the housing project yet."

"It's all in the environment, honey. When you flounder in filth and dirt, you're going to come out smelling like a pig, and when you live in a rose garden, you'll come out of that rose garden fresh as a rose."

"But, Mom, what about Barbara and Harold's baby? Will they have to stay here and live?"

"Honey, self-preservation is the key to success. We got to get ourselves together first, and then we may be able to help Barbara and little Harold. I mean, little little Harold. After all, your brother is Harold Junior, named after your daddy, so Barbara named the baby Harold the Second."

"Look at them, Mom. She's crying and waving at us with the baby. I feel so sorry for them."

"Yes, honey, but I'd feel more sorry if we had to stay here in this jungle. We lived here for over ten years, and look what all we got. Just the clothes on our backs and the rags in those borrowed suitcases. We haven't made any progress at all in the fifteen years we've lived in North Las Vegas, not one step forward."

"Maybe we can get Harold to move back here with his girlfriend and son. It's too dangerous for Barbara to be here by herself with the baby. Look at them over there across the street, watching us leave."

"I can tell you right now, Sylvia, that Harold is not moving back here. Your Uncle Harry has always lived large, child, and he has always been one to take care of family. Why, all that land and property in Atlanta that your grandparents left him was worth a fortune, child. But I still don't understand why your Uncle Harry is always running those con games on everybody. He's got plenty of money.

I guess it's part of his makeup, part of his personality, part of his compulsive behavior that gives him those inclinations to always want to cheat people."

As the cab driver shifted gears from park to drive, he politely turned off the red digital meter and radioed back to the cab station that there was a change in menu. Paula Simmons, Sylvia Simmons, and baby Cynthia were leaving the housing projects in North Las Vegas, where they had lived a good part of their lives.

"Now will you look at that, Sylvia." Paula glanced toward the mailboxes. "Just look at all those people over there, just waiting for the mailman to arrive. You can sure tell when the first of the month is here."

"Yeah, Mama. This is the only time of the month that everybody in the whole housing projects wakes up before eight in the morning and puts on their best attire to stand there in line, waiting on that mailman to deliver those welfare checks. I've seen many a fight waiting in that line at the mailbox for those welfare checks."

"Oh, here comes the mailman now, escorted by one Metro car in the front of the mail car and one Metro police car in back. Now isn't that a pitiful sight, child?"

"Look at them, Mama, fighting over a place in line, as if they were inside a boxing ring with their arms up in the air, waiting for the first punch."

"Honey, those days are over for us. We'd be right there with them, fighting alongside of them just like animals if it weren't for you."

"No, Mama, you're the one who tried to teach us right from wrong. But we were just in the wrong environment. It's because of you that we're finally realizing there's another way of life."

"Thank you, Sylvia, and thank you, Jesus!"

The driver absentmindedly listened to their conversation as he drove from North Las Vegas to Las Vegas proper. The colors of the scenery changed from black, white and housing-project grey. Instead of writing on the walls, there were shrubbery and trees. Instead of the dull grey housing project buildings, there were pastel colors and different-colored tile roofs that stimulated the mind and made the threesome more aware of the deprivation and depressing environment from which they had come. For the first time in several years, Paula cautiously reached down inside her worn and torn pocketbook and got a small cracked mirror. She began to look at herself and started to pack her hair down and brush her hair. Sylvia was surprised at the transformation in her mother's personality and looks.

"Here, Mama, let me brush your hair a little on this side. Now that's it. You look good," said Sylvia.

"Why, thank you, dear. Oh, and put a little lipstick on, honey. Not too bright, just something that will show how beautiful you are."

"Thank you, Mama. Is this a good color?"

"Yes, that will do just fine, dear. That color goes with your blouse. Now do something with your hair before we get to your Uncle Harry's house. Brush the back of it, honey."

Oh boy, the cab driver thought to himself, is old Harry in for a surprise. He's living in that ritzy area with all the high-rollers, and now he's taking in all of these low-roller relatives. Harry's life was in for a dramatic change.

As the cab driver turned on his signal to indicate a left turn onto Alta Street, Sylvia looked out the cab window in amazement. "This is Uncle Harry's house, Mama?"

"I guess so, dear. The cab driver knows your Uncle Harry, and I don't think he would be taking us to someone else's house," Paula responded.

33

"Look at the plants and trees and all the beautiful flowers! Why, this place looks like a mansion, with the driveway that circles around and the iron electric gates. I didn't know that Uncle Harry was rich!"

"Child, your Uncle Harry sold all of your dad's land in Atlanta, and this is part your house and Harold's, and, of course, the babies, both of them."

"So how come we weren't informed that the family had some money stashed away? If it belonged to us, how come we weren't there to get ours?"

"Don't you start no shit!" Paula's eyes got tight and her voice was belligerent. "Your Uncle Harry knows exactly what to do with you kids' inheritance. Besides, you would have sold this whole house by now for a twenty-dollar piece of that rock cocaine if this house were in your name, the condition you were in a few months ago. And your brother probably would have been right here in this circular driveway selling rock cocaine and got taken off to jail and got the house confiscated by the police if this house were in his name. So don't you say a word about what is rightfully yours and your brother's inheritance."

"Here we are, Mrs. Simmons. This is the last bag. Here comes your brother-in-law, Harry. Hi, Harry."

"Well, I do declare, if it ain't my little niece, Sylvia, and my sister-in-law, Paula. And look who had the pleasure of bringing my relatives home! Joe, Joe Kaplan! Thanks, Joe, and here's a little something extra for you and those grandbabies of yours." He slipped a fifty-dollar bill into Joe's hand.

"Oh, now, Harry. After all that you have done for me, I can't accept this," the cabby said, not protesting too hard.

"Well then, just put it away for when those grandbabies visit, and you can take them to the Circus arcades, Joe."

"Thanks, Harry, thanks a lot."

Either Harry was up to something or he'd flipped out, Joe Kaplan, the cab driver, thought to himself. It had been over fifteen years since he'd seen Harry, and taking in this riff-raff was just not his style.

Sure, Joe thought to himself, Harry had a family. Why, he'd been married seven times, but all those wives turned out to be duds. And old Harry had kids spread all over the world. Now he was taking in these in-laws of his. No, it didn't compute. He was up to something, getting ready to turn over some heavy cash, getting ready to make a comeback. Harry must be getting ready to "stick" one of these large casinos!

The cab driver continued to culture the thought, determined to find out what old Harry was up to. Harry was known as a risk taker, a mind regulator, when it came to putting a group of offbeat people together. He used precise timing and professional accuracy, which is what had kept old Harry around all of these years and out of jail. If all the players weren't able to play, he did not referee the game. Harry called all the shots. He was like a commanding general, and all of his troops were devoted to his commands and decisions.

Now Harry had his sister-in-law, Paula Simmons, living with him. Until recently, he hadn't given a damn about her, he had let her live in the county housing projects for all those years, never even returning her phone calls.

And then there was Harold, Harry's nephew, a clumsy nineteen-year-old petty drug pusher who had the stature and all the good looks to be another Denzel Washington. The boy had no scruples and no common sense. It would take years to train Harold to even know how to put his right and left shoe on correctly, let alone teach him about the game of "crossroading."

And Harry's niece, Sylvia. Why, she was no more than a lowlife little prostitute, using her body to get some of that rock cocaine. Harry certainly had his hands full. If he could pull this one off he deserved an Academy Award, at least a nomination.

"Oh, Mama, come and look at this furniture in the living room! Ain't it beautiful!"

"Yes, child. They call it French Provencial," said Paula.

"French what? I can't even pronounce that word, let alone imagine what he paid for all of this beautiful furniture."

"Now I told you, Sylvia, not to mention what happened to your inheritance. And stop calculating what your uncle is worth, girl. You're lucky that Uncle Harry was nice enough to give us a place to live. Harry, Harry, where is Harold?" Paula called out as Harry was placing the luggage in the different rooms that his sister-in-law and niece would be occupying.

"Harold is occupying the guest house out back. I'll call him and get the cook to serve lunch. You all make yourselves comfortable. I'll be in there in one minute."

"Mama, did you hear what Uncle Harry said? A guest house out back, a cook, our own rooms! Uncle Harry's got money. He's rich, Mama, and where were you when they were handing out our lot?"

"Child, I told you once and I'm not going to tell you again. That money belonged to your Dad's side of the family. Your Uncle Harry was the executor, and he invested every red cent of it. Now the money is finally turning over. Why, Harry pulled that money out of those savings and loans just before the market collapsed. They called it Black Friday, but Harry called it the Big Payback Day. He invested wisely, girl, and this is what his investments got him. Ain't this house beautiful?"

"Mama, why does Harold get his own house in the back? Why can't I have the house in the back since I got the baby to take care of?"

"I'll talk to your uncle about that. I think you got a point there, but maybe not, since you ain't never took care of that baby before. Knowing you, you'll be back there smoking that crack cocaine again, blowing that drug all over this baby and having big orgies. No, that's not a good idea! I got to keep my eye on you until you have fully recuperated off those drugs."

"Well, who's going to keep an eye on you, Mama? As soon as you get some money from Uncle Harry, you'll be right back at those casinos. You're not rehabilitated. And this is the Strip. The cost of gambling and the stakes are higher here. This is not downtown. Don't try to run my life, Mama. You just try to control your own compulsion to gamble!"

Oh Lord, Paula thought to herself as she moved toward Sylvia to slap her. You can take a person out of the ghetto, but you cannot take the ghetto out of the person. As she drew back her hand to smack Sylvia, Uncle Harry walked in. Sylvia trotted like a newborn filly horse toward her uncle and held him by the waist and told him how much she admired his home.

"No, Sylvia, this is our home," he said. "This house belongs to the whole family, even my children who are grown now and have their own little families. You see, this house was purchased with the money that your grandaddy and grandmother left for me and your dad. I sold the family land in Atlanta just at the right time. Since they were having the Olympics there, we got ten times the amount that land was really worth."

"I got to give it to you, Harry," Paula said. "You always

knew when to pitch a deal and when to close it—the old pitch and close technique."

"Yeah, Paula, I just happened to be fortunate in my life, but I've settled down in my old age."

"Old age? Why, if it weren't for that salt-and-pepper hair and that bicycle mustache of yours, you wouldn't look a day over thirty. I can just imagine how Harold is going to look when he gets up in age. The both of you look so much alike," Paula said.

"Well, Paula, we're from good stock, high-class people. I even traced our family roots to the time we were of royalty. Yeah, that's right, royalty. We had a whole island in Madagascar, near the Continent of Africa, and that's where we get our English features, our pointed noses and high cheekbones, that aristocratic look. And as soon as Harold learns the ropes from me, the family will be set for life."

"Learns the ropes? Harry, what are you talking about?"

"I'm teaching Harold how to be a gentleman. He even has a whole new tailored wardrobe and I've bought him a new convertible Mustang."

"Oh no, I knew it. I told Harold not to come here to live with you. I tried to get him to go back to Atlanta and go to school. Now you've taught him those old con games of yours. You're using him as a patsy."

"Sylvia, take the baby to your room on the right hand side down the hallway. Your mother and I have a few choice words to discuss."

"Let him be a patsy, Mom, whatever that is," Sylvia said as she grabbed the baby and the bag of Pampers. "He's a rich patsy, and it's better than those drugs he was dealing. At least Harold is still alive, Mama. He is a living patsy."

"Girl, go to your room and stay out of our business," said Paula sternly. She turned to her brother-in-law. "Look, Harry, I've told you over and over I don't want Harold living the lifestyle you and your brother lived years ago, all that crooked gambling and heisting. It's a wonder the mob hasn't caught up with you for those big money deals that you used to pull off. You've got a death wish, and when they come and get you I don't want my son around you."

"No, no, no, Paula. It's not like that. Why, I'm out of that game."

"No, you ain't. Don't forget, when I first moved here to Las Vegas I stayed with you off of Fremont Street when the kids were just babies. I know you, Harry. You have a compulsive behavior just like your brother. The color of money is your compulsion. The both of you would put your mother on the corner to attain more money, God bless her soul."

Harry walked over to the bar and asked Paula if she wanted a drink. He was speechless and disappointed to know what his sister-in-law really thought of him. They'd remained friends for years after the death of her husband, Harold Senior, and Harry's twin brother. "I fixed your favorite drink, Paula. You remember when Harold and I used to come a-calling after you and your sister, Denise, back in Atlanta when both of you were teenagers?"

"Yeah, Harry. Those were the good old days. But you can't fool me with all that smooth talk. I know you like the back of my hand. You and your brother were con artists then, and you're still one now. So just give me my drink and show me to my room. We'll discuss this whole thing later after I have got myself situated."

Just then Harold walked in through the double French doors in back. Paula dropped her glass on the marble floor as if she had seen a ghost. She stared at her son as he stood there tall and proud, as if he were saluting Old Glory, the red, the white, and the blue. The glass shattered on the marble floor, and the cook went to retrieve the broom and a dustpan like a retriever dog would go after a fallen duck in the wild.

"Harold, is that you? Come here to your mother. You look so handsome, just like your father. You've gotten a new haircut and new clothes. Goodness, you're handsome!"

"Hi, Mother," Harold responded, but did not embrace her. He still remembered the abuse he'd received from his mom and the argument they'd had no more than a month ago back at the housing project.

"Boy, you look like you've gotten taller, and you've put on a few pounds, too. I can see that your Uncle Harry has been taking good care of you, Son."

"Yes, Mom, I've been adjusting well here at Uncle Harry's estate."

"Listen to you. You sound like you just graduated from one of those Ivory Tower schools, Harvard or Yale. Harry, what have you done to this boy? He's the mirror image of you and your brother."

"Well, Paula, when he first arrived here I couldn't understand that language he was using. Talking that gang language, he was always flipping his hands around and repeating words such as, 'it's like this, it's like that, it's like this, you know.' I couldn't understand a word he was saying. I knew the most effective way for two men to get along with each other was to communicate effectively, so I hired Harold a tutor and bought him a new compact-disc player and purchased classical music."

"Harry, I have to give it to you. In no more than two months time you have changed my son into a prince in shining armor! I'll stay out of your business now. You're a man and Harold is a man, and it's none of my business what you do. Harold is not my little baby, now. He's a man, and a fine gentleman, I might add."

"Mother," Sylvia walked into the room. "Have you seen the baby's pacifier?" She looked over at Harold and was amazed. "Harold, is that you?"

"Hi, Sis," Harold said as Sylvia ran over to hug her brother. Tears began to flow out of Paula's eyes and Sylvia's eyes as they all embraced each other. "Why, Harold, if you weren't my big brother, I'd be trying to get with you," Sylvia said.

"That's quite enough, Sylvia!" Paula barked. "Harry, can you do something with this child? Make Sylvia into a princess, just like you made my son Harold a prince?"

"She has a ghetto mentality, Mom," Harold said. "But now that she is out of the ghetto, maybe she'll blossom and transform just like I did. Give her some time."

"We'll take care of her, Paula," Harry said as he instructed the cook to prepare lunch. "We are going shopping at the Mirage Mall today, and I am going to buy Sylvia and you a whole new wardrobe!"

*   *   *

At the Union Plaza Hotel and Casino, Joe Kaplan, the cab driver, was at the sports betting bar eyeing the satellite sports racing screen where the races were coming out of Santa Anita, California. He was thinking to himself, Hmm, if I parlay a baseball bet before one o'clock and place a bet at Santa Anita before the third race, I can come out ahead and walk out of this joint with over three hundred dollars. He was already counting his winnings.

"Hey, Joe," a voice spoke behind him. He turned to his right to face the person speaking to him.

"Why, I'll be damned. If it ain't Benny Benniola. How you been, Benny? What the hell are you doing back in Las Vegas?"

"Just taking care of a little business, Joe. How about yourself? How you been doing?"

"I've been making it, Benny. You know things aren't the same here in Las Vegas since the big machines done took over gambling," Joe said.

"What 'big machines,' Joe? And who took over Las Vegas?"

"Oh, you know. They got those young kids now, these corporate M.B.A. kids, that have taken over all the odds of winning. The odds are stacked against us. Even the old man, Jack Daughn, has retired, and his son Junior has taken over this joint, the Union Plaza. Why, we can't even get credit. Junior runs this place like a business, like one of those Fortune 500 businesses. Everything is done by computer. Even the slot machines are computer operated now. We ain't got no chance of winning. I stopped gambling, Benny."

"Well, what's that in your hand? It looks like a duck and quack, like a parlay card. Did you get a tip on a bet, Joe?"

"Nope, just reminiscing about the old days of being a runner and placing those bets for the bosses and I just happened to pick up a card here."

"Speaking of the bosses and runners, have you seen or heard from Harry, Harry Simmons?"

"Yeah, I hear from him every now and then. But you know I am not one to discuss anybody's business, personal or private, as that's what's been keeping me alive all of these years."

"Well, he contacted old Louie, and Louie gave me the message that Harry had some work for me, so I flew in from Chicago."

"I knew it! I just knew old Harry was up to his old tricks again. He's got a big estate over off Alta, around the corner from Jerry Lewis's old estate near Rancho. What the both of you got going, Benny?"

"Well, I'm just like you, Joe. I don't ask questions and I don't go inquiring about other people's business. Check you out later, Joe. Hey, Joe, I got a tip on the third race at Santa Anita. Bet on the Hammer—a sure win."

"Thanks, Benny. Hey, you think Harry needs any backup, I mean, just like the old days? I'm still part of the family, aren't I?"

"Yeah, Joe, you were a hell of a good driver then, and you're still a hell of a guy. But you can't kiss and tell, Joe. You got to keep your mouth shut no matter what goes down. I'll talk to Harry this evening and get back with you."

"Thanks, Benny. And hey, I'd appreciate it if you can give Harry a good word or two for me. You know I have six grandkids now, and they love that new water slide at the Circus Hotel, but the damn thing costs money."

"Yeah, I know. They're making Vegas the new Disneyland for kids, making those kids compulsive players already. Those corporate machines from Harvard and Yale and Berkeley are indoctrinating those kids on the compulsive techniques of gambling, and we're going to put a stop to it, Joe. Harry and me."

Benny Benniola was well known in Las Vegas years ago as the Master of the Slot Machine. He devised a plan to rip off every major casino slot machine some fifteen years ago by using a mold that duplicated the slot machine key and then later sending a few of his confederates into the casino to win million dollar jackpots by

43

opening up the slot machine and adjusting the wheels. The Wheel of Fortune, he called his plan. Unfortunately, he was caught and run out of Las Vegas by the mob when one of his confederates skipped out on him, fearing for his life. That confederate was later found in the Mojave Desert, dead as a doornail, and Benny was accused of murder.

There's something in the air, Joe thought to himself. Why would Benny risk his life by coming back to Las Vegas after all of these years? Harry hadn't scored a good lick in years, and now all of a sudden he was spending money like it was his last days on Earth, moving all those relatives in with him and comping Benny a room here at the Plaza.

Well, whatever went down, he hoped Benny would count him in. These guys were professional crossroaders, and they didn't make mistakes, Joe thought to himself. Besides, these were rough times, and even an old pro like himself could use some extra cash.

4

"You mean to tell me that this is the first time that you've been on the Strip in Las Vegas, Sylvia?"

"Yes, Harry. Living in the ghetto all those years was like living in prison. With our finances we couldn't even think about leaving North Las Vegas, let alone coming over to the Las Vegas Strip where all the fine restaurants and the rich people go to gamble."

"Paula, why didn't you let me know your financial situation was so severe? You know you could have called on me?"

"Well, Harry, you know how I am. I'm not one to impose on others. Besides, we adjusted and we survived."

"Yeah, we survived, all right," Harold said and he drove down the Strip. "But there's plenty of battle scars, emotional and psychological."

"Things will be a lot different now. Pull up here at Caesar's Hotel, Harold, and let's do some shopping at the new Caesar's Mall."

It was embarrassing the way Paula and Sylvia acted, like they were in Disneyland for the first time. They started grabbing and trying on clothes, talking too loud, bumping into people. They were primitive, but having a good time, and Harry let them shop to their heart's content, purchasing the best of clothing for his niece and sister-in-law. Part of it was that he sort of felt badly about the money he'd received after selling the family home in Atlanta and not giving the kids their share. Part of it was maybe he was plotting something and needed the confidence and support of his family. These three were the only family he had left. His own kids had deserted him due to his compulsive schemes and scams.

Paula knew there must be some underlying reason, but she wasn't going to ask any questions, not yet at least. She was having too much of a good time, shopping and seeing another side of life. She was like a kid again.

"Uncle Harry, how do you think this dress looks on me?"

"It looks good, Sylvia. I didn't know you even had a shape until now. That dress brings out the woman in you, and those shoes will sure finish off any doubts that you're not a little girl any more."

Harold came over with a concerned look. "Let's not spend all of Uncle Harry's money. You and Mom have already charged up over a thousand dollars in dresses and other stuff."

"Look who's talking! I don't hear you complaining about that new convertible Mustang Uncle Harry bought you. Let's go tell Uncle Harry to return it. Tell him it's too expensive, and you would prefer a bicycle."

"I work for what I have, girl. Uncle Harry just co-signed for me and put the money down out of the money I earned working for him," Harold said angrily.

"Worked for it? What kind of work have you done? Why, I haven't seen you work since you left the ghetto, where you was selling that 'candy' on the street corner in the projects. That's the only work I ever saw you do, if you can call that work. Sure, you turned over a few dollars a night, but you were too busy reinvesting that money, trying to be some high-roller with a tight budget."

"Well, things are different now. I'm working for Uncle

46

Harry. I'm his right-hand man."

"Mama told me about Uncle Harry and the things he used to do in his younger days, so you be careful, Harold. Don't get too deep into what Uncle Harry does. That little boy you fathered back in the junkie jungle will never get a chance to see his daddy if you aren't careful."

"You mean Barbera," Harold said.

"Yeah. We met her, me and Mama."

"Mama know who she is?"

"Yes, she used to come over all the time with that cute little baby, my nephew."

"I wonder why Mama hasn't said anything to me about the baby and Barbera. That's strange."

"She thought you were gay all these years, Harold, since you never once brought a girl over. That time she caught you behind that building with that slime queen sucking your dick, well, she didn't know what to think."

"I'm not like you, Sylvia. I don't go around with a lot of different people. Besides, there's too many diseases out there. You should be more careful about who you're fuckin'."

"That's what they got rubbers for. Haven't you ever used one, Harold?"

"That's why they got AIDS. Ain't you heard of AIDS, Sylvia? Because of promiscuity, AIDS is taking a lot of peoples' lives."

"Yeah, gay people like yourself, not heterosexuals like me."

"I'm not gay, I'm just careful. You better have an AIDS test done. I don't want to get the virus by sitting on the toilet or using the same bathtub as you."

"Fool, that's not how you get AIDS. AIDS is contracted by sex or by blood transfusions. It's through the blood, not through breathing or skin."

47

"Yeah, I know that. I just wanted to pick at you and find out what you really know about it. After all, you're still my little sister and I got to take care of you."

"Harold, you can take care of me by getting me some drugs."

"No! I thought you were off that stuff," Harold said angrily. "You've gained some weight back and you're looking like a human being again. You don't need any more drugs."

"I was just teasing you, Harold, to see if you gone back to your old ways," said Sylvia and they both laughed. But they both hid in that compulsive behavior, that urge, that physiological feeling of wanting a quick fix to gratify their needs, their wants.

"The last time I was ever on the Las Vegas Strip was in 1978 when I worked at the Stardust Hotel," Paula explained as they returned home from their shopping spree. "The glamor and joy of dancing, and the feeling of being wanted and noticed was one of the high points of my life. We did a show three times a night wearing all the beautiful colors and feathers, just like Josephine Baker did in France, but not so revealing."

"Mama, did you dance nude?"

"Oh no, Sylvia, just half nude," Paula explained.

"Maybe that's why I always wanted to take off all my clothes and dance, Mama. Sometimes I just get the urge to be free and not have anything smothering my body. Maybe I get that from you."

"No, child, probably from your father's side of the family, but not from me," Paula said hastily.

"That's probably how that baby popped up," Harold joked.

Paula continued. "That was when we first moved here from California. You two were just babies, and we lived with your Uncle Harry in a cheap motel off of Paradise Road. The lights, the people, and the lure of all that money is what got me hooked on gambling. I wanted something better for you children, and the only way for me to get a better life was gambling—or at least that's the way I saw it back then. The menfolks were always trying to take me to bed since I was the only colored girl in the show and they thought I was vulnerable and needed their money. But I never even entertained the thought, and I came straight home to look after you young ones every night when I got off work. Every morning I was there to send you two off to school.

"I was finally fired because I wouldn't give in. Those men were ruthless animals. My only enjoyment was playing those slots. I became a slot machine junkie. Oh, I got a few good payoffs, but those payoffs only made things worse for me. That fifteen-second gratification, that pay-off when those colorful cherries all lines up . . . that sound, that music, those bells a-ringin' was fine music to my ears, child. I was somebody then, I was a star. I was a fool to put all my winnings back into that damn machine. But you know, it wasn't even the money I was playing for after that big win. It was for that climax, that gratification, that sensation I got from that big win that first time. I reached my peak and I wanted that feeling over and over again."

"It's like bungie jumping, Mama, that feeling you get from bungie jumping. It feels great!"

"No, Harold, it's like taking a big blast of rock cocaine. That's how I got hooked," said Sylvia. "That first try, that first experiment with that rock cocaine. Mama, I ain't never had a feeling like that again."

"Child, I hope you never have a feeling like that again. You could have died from those drugs, like that basketball player, Len Bias."

49

"We all have different compulsions in life," said Harry, "and I'm not afraid to admit to the three of you that my compulsion isn't drugs or gambling, not even winning with the horses. My compulsion is making that grand slam, getting off from ripping off. After seeing how these big casinos rip off so many people, I had a compulsion, a desire, a need to rip these casino owners off for every penny they got. Just look at those homeless people over there." Harry pointed out two men holding up signs stating they needed money and food.

"Those homeless people are standing right in front of the Mirage Casino, a casino that made a profit of sixty-eight million dollars last year. Combined with all these casinos, over 150 billion dollars throughout the world of total profit was made. It's a damn shame that there are homeless people hungry and they have nowhere to live."

"Maybe he has a compulsion to be a bum," Harold said.

"Maybe so, son, but we'll leave that up to the sociologists and psychiatrists to figure out."

"Yes," Paula commented, "Las Vegas has quite a history, and if I'd known that this place is a mobster's paradise, I would never have come here. Those with money will always find a sucker in every corner to make a quick buck, and that's what keeps these casinos operating. Suckers, kids. And the State of Nevada allows this riff-raff here. The Nevada State Tax Commission is getting the palm of their hand squeezed royally just by allowing this racketeering to happen. This place ain't nothing but a haven for con artists, high-rollers and money laundering!

"Watch out, Harold! That car just about hit us! That fool almost hit us, and he was going as far as to that casino to lose his little money. You see what I mean, kids? This place is full of compulsive personalities, and there aren't enough churches, psychiatrists, and sociologists to help these poor souls. This place is a big playground for them to cheat, steal and rob each other blind. It's nothing but a little state where the United States allows a place for the mob to live. Just leave the rest of us alone; you got Vegas, mob. Leave us the rest of the nation.

"They all need to be cured, but it's an incurable disease. That's what they figured when they allowed this place to exist. It's Compulsive Behavior Land!" Paula shouted in disgust.

"Paula's right," said Harry. "This is the playground of the mob. Why, a family man can't even afford to give his wife and kids a decent vacation here in Las Vegas these days. The cost has skyrocketed, and the subliminal techniques they use to lure the suckers in work every time.

"There was a story in the newspaper about a man from Montana who drove out here with his family—three kids and his wife—years ago on a vacation one cold winter to get away from that dreadful snow. He lost everything he had—his money, his car, the deeds to his farm and his house. He never knew he was a closet compulsive gambler. He got a one-time big win and then lost all of that money back. Then he kept trying to regain his losses, then asked for credit to try to get home back to Montana and signed a marker. A marker is a contract made by you to the casino that you'll repay the money or they use gangster tactics to get their money back.

"Well, that man from Montana signed several markers and lost every single thing he had in the world. He had to depend on Public Assistance to shelter himself and his family. When his father finally sent him some money to catch a bus home, he gambled that, too. His wife and children left him in Las Vegas, where he still lives, at the St. Vincent de Paul shelter for the homeless. He couldn't kick the habit. He's a classic compulsive gambler."

Paula interrupted, "Harry is right, kids. Right over there is where that gangster, Bugsy Siegel, built the fabulous Flamingo Hilton, from the mob money, and never got a chance to see its completion. He was gunned down in Beverly Hills, a hit from another mob gang."

"That's right," confirmed Harry. "I got the movie *Bugsy,* starring, oh what's his name, Shirley McLaine's brother, uh, George Hamilton."

"No, not George Hamilton," Paula interrupted. "It's Beatty, Warren Beatty. It's a great movie. That movie explains how this place got off the ground, kids. Gambling isn't just in Las Vegas, either. There's gambling all over this nation. In New Jersey there are gambling casinos, and all over the nation there are Indian tribes raking in money from bingo games. Even in Mississippi there is a boat that carries passengers from one end of the river to the other end, and all they do is gamble. It's a large casino boatload of compulsive gamblers.

"Anything that's excessive leads to compulsion, and some people are more susceptible to compulsiveness. That's what I learned by attending a Gamblers' Anonymous meeting, where they ran down the psychological and physiological reasons of what they call 'a disorder of impulse control.' It's the same thing found in most drug users. Are you listening, Sylvia?"

"Mama, I ain't got nothing to say. I got a new compulsion, and that's shopping at the mall."

5

Each of them subconsciously thought to themselves as they drove south on the Las Vegas Strip about how they could get over on the other. Life was too short, too critical, and too good to be true for them now. Paula, Harold, and Sylvia Simmons could not go back to the ghetto to live among the junkies in North Las Vegas. They'd do what they had to to stay where they were.

Paula thought to herself, Harry and I have to talk. I can't figure what he's up to, but I know him. He's going to get these kids of mine in a hell of a mess with his high-rolling and crossroading at these here casinos. Just look at him. He's probably calculating how much he's just spent on us and trying to figure out what kind of return he's going to get. He's a con artist and a professional shyster, and that compulsive behavior is in his blood.

Uncle Harry is setting me up for life, thought Harold. I just know these two bitches are going to fuck up my shit, and then I'll be back in that hell hole. I know it's my mom and my baby sister, and I love them, but the game here is self-preservation. I know damn well if I make it, I'll pull them through. I got to talk to Harry tonight and convince him to send the "bitches' brew" back to the bottom or my ass will end up "frying" by those loansharks that invested in this scheme!

Harold sure has matured since last time I saw him, Sylvia thought to herself. He's got a convertible Mustang and he thinks he's rolling. Maybe he can roll back to the old block and get me some cocaine tonight. I need a blast real bad, and I can just kick back at Harry's pad and imagine I'm shopping at the mall with a million dollars of Uncle Harry's money, or having sex sitting on a toilet stool. That's what that drug used to make me feel like doing. I don't care who knows it, I need that drug more than I need a man, more than I need my family. I'll have to find a way to blackmail Harold into getting me some more drugs, or think of some excuse for him to take me back to the old neighborhood.

Operation Parlay is coming along just fine, Harry thought. I have four players lined up already, and I know I can trust three of them. Paula will make a fine decoy when we wire up those slot machines from this end of the Las Vegas Strip to the Sahara Hotel. And we'll have Sylvia and Harold work the downtown area. I got to get the both of them some I.D. cards and some uniforms, and then it'll be a piece of cake. My crew will be getting in from Chicago and Philadelphia by tomorrow, and everything else will be just like clockwork.

"You see that hotel there, kids? The Flamingo Dunes Hotel and Casino? That's where your mother and auntie used to work years ago as cocktail waitresses."

"Yeah, Harry, I can still remember the Dunes just like it was yesterday."

"It's closing down now, and they're converting it to a water park," Harry mentioned.

"Old Lady Esther lived on the eleventh floor of the Dunes for over fourteen years, and now she has to finally move," Paula remarked.

"Fourteen years?" said Sylvia. "She lived in a casino for fourteen years?"

"That's right. Her husband left her a fortune, but she

figured why stay in a large mansion when she could be accommodated by room service and all that amenities just by staying at the Dunes. It worked out for her for the last fourteen years, but now they're selling everything. Some wealthy Japanese purchased the Dunes for over a hundred fifty million dollars and ended up selling it to the Mirage Corporation for seventy-five million—a steal if I ever saw one. That old lady was the only one who bene-fitted. Why, it took the Brinks truck three days to take all of her money out of her hotel suite. She hid the money in some of the strangest places," chuckled Harry.

"Whatever happened to Aunt Diane, your sister?" asked Harold.

"Well, your Aunt Diane was just the opposite of me," said Paula. "She took risks and was into the Mafia lifestyle, always dating and taking money from those gangsters. She ran plenty of games and made plenty of money, but one day it all caught up with her. She got caught in the Chicago mob and talked a little too much and tried to get in a little too deep into their money laun-dering and drug distributing. Then it happened. She was set up and was found dead in the Mojave Desert."

"She got into it a little bit too deep for all of us," said Harry. "We tried to help her, but she had this compulsive need and desire for more. She was a call girl for the Mafia, and made over a thousand dollars a night. But she got greedy. She tried to blackmail a big boss mob member, threatening to call his wife and expose him. The next thing we knew, your Aunt Diane was found dead in the sand."

"Harold, can you stop for a few minutes at the Star-dust? I just want to go in and see if a few friends of mine are still working there," said Paula.

"No, Mom. Uncle Harry and I got to make a few busi-ness runs. You ain't got no friends at the Stardust. At least none that are human. That slot machine ain't your friend, Mom, it's your worst nightmare. So don't try those old games on me, lying and crying on my shoulder the next day when you lost all of your money. I saw Uncle Harry give you that hundred-dollar bill. You better keep it, because you're going to need a place to live."

Paula slapped him hard. "Ow! Why did you slap me? I almost wrecked the car! You're just afraid to hear the truth, Mama. I wouldn't tell you anything but the truth, because I love you and I love Sis. But you hate me and always treated me bad. You always saw Dad in me. I remember how you used to beat me and call out *his* name—yes, you did. You hated him because he ran off with another woman. You were just too ignorant for Dad and too dominant. I was just five years old, but I can still remember the fights you both used to have, breaking dishes and yelling. Dad left you just like I did, because you're a yellow-skinned bitch who always thought you were better than everybody else. If you don't move from Uncle Harry's house, then I will. I ain't going to have you beat up on me anymore."

"Oh, Harold, I'm so sorry, but you know you just don't show me any respect, and I've always told you that. You just drive me back to the house, and I'll catch a cab."

Now's my chance to play on Harold's sympathy, Sylvia thought to herself, and then he'll take me to get some drugs. If I play Harold against Mama, Harold will give me anything. "Mama, Harold is a grown man, and you got to stop hitting him upside the head. Why, that's probably why he's so dumb. Just look at him, Mama." Harold had cut his hair real close and got rid of that baseball cap that he used to put on sideways. His clothes fit him as if he hired a tailor to sew them. "He's lookin' good, Mama, so get off his back."

"That's true, Sylvia, your brother has made a dramatic change. He looks so handsome, and he's finally doing something positive for himself, so I can't complain about that. I'm sorry, Harold, and I'll never hit you in the head again."

"Don't hit me anywhere, because the next time you do, I'm gonna break your arm."

"Here, here, you two. You both kiss and make up. You two put me back to when my brother and you were married, Paula. The both of you used to fight like cats and dogs, and I can see the same thing happening again. You both are all you've got, so let's be more like family and love one another."

"Okay, Uncle Harry. Sorry, Mom."

"Sorry, Harold. I love you, but you got to give me some respect. You have something against women that I just can't figure out. You seem to hate women, and I hope that don't stem from me."

"No, I love you, Mom. And I love certain women, the ones with money."

That's when Paula was certain that Harry had influenced her son and groomed him to take over his throne as the King of the Crossroaders. Harold had been trained that the only value in life was money. The only thing in his life was not in the shape of a woman's beautiful figure, but of those dollars measuring six inches across and three inches wide. Harry had him, lock, stock and barrel, and there wasn't a damn thing she could do about it. The boy was nineteen years old, going on forty, now, and full of game. It was in his genes, "something" that he'd inherited from his father's side of the family. That "something" would get him killed if he wasn't careful.

Advising and talking to Harold became impossible. It was as if he had a death wish, a compulsion to put himself into a situation to be killed, and the only gratification that he got out of it was the element of escaping alive. Harold was a daredevil just like his dad—and a fool.

Back home from the shopping mall, Harry begin to think about his big plan. "The whole is greater than its parts," was one of the rules Harry had heard from his first psychology class at UNLV. When you got his ignorant relatives together, they acted like monkeys in a zoo. It was going to take a miracle to pull off this heist. But what else were these three morons good for? They were his people, his flesh and blood, but their environmental influences, living in the ghetto where there were homicides and drug deals every day, had its effect on them. The only thing he could do was use them as patsies in Operation Parlay. He would place them in positions to distract and act as confederates in the scam. It was the only way.

By the time Harry and the others had arrived home, three of the Parlay players had made contact, leaving messages that they were staying at the Union Plaza Hotel in downtown Las Vegas. Sammy, an illusionist at the game of blackjack, was the best of the bunch, known throughout the gambling world in such places as New Jersey and Vegas. Sammy used the old "hat trick" to put the blackjack dealers at the casinos in a state of mystery. He would go into a casino, place a bet for five hundred dollars a hand, and slip several blackjack wins in right before the eyes of the card dealers. Sammy used anything to create an illusion—a big, flashy diamond ring reflecting off the lights gave Sammy just enough time to slip another ace and king from under his sleeves into the deck of cards. Or he'd spill a drink and slip in a nine for a double-down bet when he had a face card down and a two showing on top, or a face card (ten) down and any card that would permit him to receive a hit to capture a perfect twenty-one at the blackjack table. Sammy was recognized at the major casinos and restricted from entering and playing blackjack, since he could win thousands of dollars by deception and illusionary card shuffling.

After Harry checked his messages, he told Paula, "Please excuse me and Harold. We have to make an unexpected run downtown, but we should be back before dinner."

"Harry," Paula said abruptly, "you're not getting Harold into something he won't be able to get out of, are you?"

"No, Paula, for heaven's sakes, no. I'm just going to introduce Harold to a few old acquaintances of mine."

"You're up to something, and I can tell because I see your mustache going up and down. Whenever that happens, you're either scheming on something or you're about to make some big money. Your nerves are giving you away, Harry. Now, what's going on?"

"Well, I didn't want to tell you this, but I have a perfect plan, the perfect scheme, the hit that will gross us over eight million dollars."

"Eight million dollars! What the hell are you going to do, rob a bank?"

"No, I'm going to exchange some capital with a few corporate executives, that's all."

"I knew it! I knew you were up to those same old tricks again, always robbing someone for their life's work. Can't you get it through your thick head that you can't get away with all that old scheming and cheating? This is 1996, and they got surveillance cameras, detectives and alarm systems. So how do you think you're going to have some of those Fortune 500 corporate executives hand you over eight million dollars? Do you think I was born yesterday? Maybe Harold was born yesterday, but not me."

"My plan will work. Why, it's my life's work. I started planning this over six years ago, gathering computer data, taking classes at UNLV, purchasing computer equipment and slot machines. This one will work. Besides, what else do we have to live for these days? The big bosses have taken over Las Vegas. They're not like the Mafia, Paula. They're meaner and have no understanding whatsoever. The big bosses who run Las Vegas today rely only on that market, and they treat everybody, even women and children, as a commodity.

"They think how much money they can make by putting in a new water slide for the kids, just to draw the adults to Las Vegas. How much money will they gain in clear profit by hiring a new circus act and a few exotic tigers and gorillas? How much more money will they gain in clear profit by building an amusement park with lots of games for the kids and lots of rides and fun for the entire family? Those corporate executives control Las Vegas now, Paula, and they only rely on statistics and not the human sacrifices.

"What do they care if two or three men got killed while building that new hotel, the Luxor? Why, if it was up to them, they'd just pour cement over them and act like it never happened. Maybe in a few hundred years, those men may get dug up, and then the stock will go sky high because those corporate heads' great-grandkids will profit, knowing that the media will publicize it and say a few mummies were found at the Luxor Pyramid, get your tickets right away. They don't give a damn, Paula. They're inhuman."

"You're the one who doesn't give a damn. You're going to feed my son to the lions. Did you think I'm not going to ask about what he's doing and where he's getting all this money? You got to be crazy!"

"Paula, in reality he was already fed to the lions when they stopped those programs that helped kids through school. He was fed to the lions when they stopped Affirmative Action. He was fed to the lions when you and the kids had to move into a housing project and stayed there all those years, with no attempt at getting you people trained at a job. Yes, Harold and a whole generation of our youth were fed to the lions years ago when the Republicans took office and stole everything they could steal in those savings and loan scams. There's no money left, Paula. They hoarded everything and gave President Clinton a billion-dollar debt."

"Clinton will make a way out of nowhere for us poor people, just you wait and see. Besides, what do you need more money for? You're living like a Greek tycoon with this house and fancy cars. What do you need more for?"

"It's not the money. It's the satisfaction of exposing those corrupt thieves of the night. Those corporate executives got their degrees from Harvard and Berkeley, and now they've got a license to push those computer buttons and make money. I can see there's no sense talking to you, Paula. Your mind is made up and you're not going to change it. I'll call a cab and have them take you and the rest of your family home to the housing projects."

"Oh no, Harry, please don't do that! We can't move back there!"

"I have no choice, Paula. I'm going through with Operation Parlay with you or without you. There will be a lot of traffic coming in and out of the house, and some of those people don't want to be seen by anybody. You either have to go back to the projects or find a room somewhere."

"It'll cost us a fortune! Four people in one of those sleazy hotel rooms in downtown Vegas. Why, you got to be kidding! Harry, if your plan is foolproof and if we're not in jeopardy of being killed or put in prison, I may decide by tomorrow if we want in. Well, not directly in, but of some help somehow to your so-called Operation Parlay."

"Fantastic!" Harry jumped up and hugged Paula. "It'll be just like the old days when it was Harold Senior and your sister Diane. But this time things will work out for us. I know they will. They must!"

Paula had decided that she and the kids would be more at risk by moving back into the housing projects where homicides and drug dealing was rampant. She couldn't take any more chances with the lives of her loved ones, Sylvia and Harold and her granddaughter. When they'd first moved into Harry's house, she remembered the looks in their eyes of hope and joy, something she couldn't give them. And Harold, he'd matured and grown so much by living with Harry for just a few months. He'd become a man, and her only hope was that Sylvia would become a lady.

"Just what is this Operation Parlay and how will I be able to make a few dollars off this big corporate takeover?"

"You'll be a confederate."

"A what?"

"A confederate, someone who is just there blocking the sight or obscuring the action that's going down. I'll clue you in on it later, but for now Harold and I have to get to the Union Plaza Hotel."

6

"Uncle Harry, just look at all the lights and colors! The people look as if they're having a great time, too," Harold exclaimed.

"Looks are deceiving, son." Harry watched for his contact to come down to the lobby while Harold looked at all of the people, seemingly having a good time. "Half of those people have severe problems and crave to put themselves at risk, son. The risk they take is a lot like a bungie jumper. It gives them a sense of omnipotence, a loss for a brief period of time of their worries, and then they act like little children until all of their money is gone. Then the harsh world of reality comes crashing down on them."

"Just listen to those slot machines, Uncle Harry. Those sounds are just like in the arcade. I know that sensation; it's one of power, the feeling of controlling that arcade machine—man against machine."

"You're right, Harold. It is the same feeling those machines give you. Those points at the arcades are similar to these machines. These gambling machines give you money, all right, but they also give you a peak experience. You reach a threshold when you know you've won, and that glorious sound penetrates your ears and hits the gratification mechanism of your brain. You hear those sounds from the time you're a kid, and that's what keeps Las Vegas in business. You have power at that arcade machine, and these people are sensing power through their sensory mechanisms, too. They feel they're in control, and for that moment they're wallowing happily in the fantasy of possessing unlimited power.

"Look at them at those slot machines, practically having an orgasm through loss of thought and concern about time and space. This is a place to get away from all your worries and sorrow, at least until you get out the front door of the casino, and then the harsh wind of reality slaps you right in the face and brings you back to your senses. By that time it's too late. All of your money is gone, and you have to find a way to survive for the rest of the week, or at least until you get more money to gamble it all away again.

"Harold, did you know there are over 23 million compulsive gamblers just in the United States alone, and you can find them in every city in the nation—betting furiously on horse races, basketball games, poker hands, bingo. They have a fever, a virus, and nothing seems to matter to them."

"I know. Mom was a slot machine junkie, and nothing else seemed to matter to her. She'd stay out all night. Sylvia and I thought she had a boyfriend, but we were wrong. She had several boyfriends, and they were jealous lovers. Those slot machines were her boyfriends, and they took her for everything."

"You know, Harold, the biggest and best customers of these casinos are their employees? They start off wagering their tip money, and pretty soon start spending their salaries. Later they might steal from the casino just to make that one last bet, the one that'll make them or break them. Chances are that last bet will break them."

"It's an illness. Those lights, those sounds and sensations that you get—they're the symptoms of the disease. Like Sylvia. She'd want a hit off of that pipe, and smoke that crack cocaine until she dropped dead. She can't resist it and might even kill for it."

"Many people have been killed for not paying off a gambling debt. Drugs and gambling are a symbiotic relationship; they both lead you straight to the grave faster than lightning striking you. If you're stupid enough to just stand out there in a storm, then that lightning bolt will strike you, it'll take your money, and it'll stop your heart from ticking."

Harry noticed Benny and Sammy coming past the gift shop at the Union Plaza. "Now, don't say a word. Let me do all the talking. Matter of fact, here's a few dollars. Just go and play that dollar slot machine, and I'll call you over and introduce you as soon as I talk to them a few minutes."

"But I'm not twenty-one yet. I can't play the slots."

"Just go over there and sit down for a few minutes and look like you're playing the slots."

Benny, the dice man, was an expert at trading off dice at the dice table, placing dice on the table that could only roll sevens, or sixes. Sammy was a master of illusion, and could flip a card so fast off the table and place a winning card in his hand to make a perfect twenty-one that the dealer didn't even realize what had happened.

"What took you so long?" Harry asked.

"Well, it's been a long time, Harry. We wanted to check out the scenery a little," Benny said.

"You'll have plenty of time to check out the scenery when we finish our work."

"And what work is that?" asked Sammy.

"The regular job, just like the old days," Harry answered.

"Things aren't like the old days, Harry. Things have

changed. Everything's run by a master computer now, and there are cameras and all kinds of surveillance all over these casinos. Besides, you and I are both too old to be going to the slammer," Sammy said.

"That's the reason I called you two. You're the best, pioneers and experts at your game, and all that we needed besides that was training in higher skills, higher technology, computer training and inside information on the transfer of funds by those computers," said Harry.

"And I suppose you have all those skills, right, Harry?"

"Yes, as a matter of fact. And if I don't, I can get it fast. Let's all go to my place and discuss this. You both know I'm not supposed to be seen in places like this."

"Okay, Harry. You're calling the shots, just like the old days. Let's go."

As Harry tried to get his nephew's attention at the slot machine, he noticed a commotion and lights and bells ringing. Harold was trying to get his uncle's attention, but a crowd had gathered. Harold had won the $2500 jackpot at the slot machine and was trying to signal him, knowing he wouldn't be able to collect the money since he was underage.

"Damn, he must be the luckiest kid in the world. Sammy, see that kid over there? Create an illusion and slip him this fake I.D. It was his father's, Harold Senior, and they look a lot alike . . . maybe he can get away with it."

Sammy created a distraction that drew the crowd to the sports betting area by yelling and hollering as if his horse was just about to come in. The people were so gullible that they joined in with him, just like a wave at a football stadium. The false identification was slipped to Harold.

The manager asked Harold a few questions and then asked him for some identification and a Social Security number. Harold gave him the false identification of his father's and used a fictitious Social Security number. He got the money and was comped by the club manager. Harold left quickly out the side door without returning to the slot machines, and hurried to his car in the valet parking. The four of them sped off to Harry's house. As they sped away, Harold was smiling about his winning at the lucky slot machine.

"Sammy, Benny, this is my son, oh, I mean my nephew, Harold. You both remember his father and my brother, Harold Senior."

"I sure do. He looks a lot like his father. And how is Paula?" asked Sammy.

"She's fine. She and her daughter, Sylvia, are living with Harold and I," Harry said as they drove down the main street toward the Las Vegas Strip.

"Hasn't this place changed? Look at the new Golden Nugget Hotel! All that marble and gold. They must have spent a fortune on just the outside of the building, let alone the inside."

"Yeah," Harry said. "The new breed has taken over most of the casinos. Now they're all run by corporate heads and corporate money. The Big Machines, boys, those M.B.A.'s at Yale and Harvard, grads run everything now, and they use statistics to project how much winnings they'll receive. The good times and the fun is all over. Las Vegas is a business now, and it's run like a business, from the roulette tables to the horse racing. There are no more breaks. It's just business."

"Why, all the privately owned casinos have gone out of business. I guess the casino operators couldn't pull off that tax avoidance gimmick like the big boys, and the taxes have skyrocketed for the casino owners," Benny replied.

"Yeah. And now there are cameras on all the tables, one camera run by the casino owner to watch the employees, and the other camera run by the Internal Revenue Service and the State of Nevada to watch the owners. It's a big racket, one eye on the other eye. There's no way anyone can get away with the stuff we used to pull," Sammy said.

"No, that's where you're wrong," said Harry. "There is a new way, and I'll explain it to you in detail when we get to my place."

"Is it okay to discuss all of this with the kid?"

"Yes. It's in his blood. He knows the golden rule."

"Yeah, right—and that rule is there's no honor among thieves," Benny replied. "Gambling, sex, excitement, plenty of fun. Once that's gone, there will be no more Las Vegas, Nevada, Harry. Why, they're building these water parks for the kids and these giant amusement parks. Look at the one over there—a giant water slide that the parents can drop the kids off at and then go gamble their lives away. That's amusing, huh?"

"Sure is, Benny, but it's also a lot of fun. You should see the one they're building at the new MGM Hotel and Casino. It's huge!"

"Gambling will always be around," Benny said as he lit up his cigar. "Why, do you know that all over the world people gambled? In Naples, those singing gondoliers staked their liberty for a certain number of years for gambling debts. The Indians in the New World cut off their fingers to pay a debt, and they also had a crude form of roulette, spinning a stick and the person to whom it fell was the winner. Even the English had crude ways of paying a debt, and that was by hanging. The winner could hang the loser." He exhaled a large, smelly puff of smoke from his cigar.

"Yes, Harold, now you've been indoctrinated with your first win, just like the first time you had good sex. You'll always try to do it again—win, win, and win some more. Get good sex, and you want it more and more and more. It's that instant of pure gratification that you get, and those mechanisms of relief are centered around the brain's mechanisms of pleasure, the pleasure syndromes. Like sex, you're going to want to gamble again and again. But I'm not sure which is more deadly, sex or gambling. Both can kill you!" Harry said.

"Listen to your uncle, son. Why, he's the King of the Crossroaders, and he knows every game in life right-side up, upside down. But be careful because, just like Benny gave you a brief history of gambling, I'm going to tell you that some gamblers risk everything, even their families. Gambling can make you a slave. In history, in China, the rice paddy workers bet their ears, and the losers sliced them off with a polite kowtow. In every age the gambling debt was a debt of honor and had to be repaid."

"Enough history of the past of Las Vegas. We're in the present now," said Harry as they arrived home. "Come on in and I'll fix both of you your favorite drinks."

Paula greeted them at the door. "Oh, my word, if it ain't Benny and Sammy. How have you two been?"

"Fine, Paula. It looks like you haven't changed in all these years," Benny responded.

"She doesn't look a day over twenty," said Sammy as the two walked into the den.

"Fix the regular for me, Harry," called Benny.

"Yeah, that goes for me, too," Sammy said as they sat down in the den. "So, Harry, tell us about this plan. You've been leading us on about this big heist, and from the phone call I could sure hear you talking, but I couldn't see you, if you know what I mean."

All hustlers in the game know the golden rule, and that is not to disclose anything over the telephone, not even to your mother, since there is usually a tail on them by some law enforcement agency, whether it's the Internal Revenue Service or the FBI.

"Yeah, Harry, the way you describe it, this will be the biggest heist since that there French Connection. Now come on, out with it," Sammy said.

"Come on into the game room and I'll give you the details. These walls may have ears, and we ain't doing nothing but talking loud and saying nothing."

"Okay, I want to see some more of your estate. It looks like you've been doing good, damn good, for yourself," said Benny.

As they walked through the house, they admired the fine china and porcelain and mirrors, the furniture and luxurious carpet. The house spoke of taste and elegance.

In the game room there were old pictures of the Dunes Hotel, along with video games and a pool table. As the three looked out at the back portion of the estate, they saw a full-length Olympic swimming pool flickering and gleaming in the moonlight, the blue water representing serenity and peace.

Paula had to find out what was about to take place back there in the game room. Her life was at stake, her kids' lives were at risk, and all her dreams of some day leaving that deprived environment for good were on the line. She was out of the junkie jungle and couldn't go back, not after smelling the fresh roses at Harry's house. She never wanted to wake up in a panic after a cockroach or a rat had crawled across her. Paula kept her eye on the door as she smelled the awful cigars that Benny smoked. They reminded her of some fifteen years ago when times had been different and when her sister was still alive and they used to be dazzling girls of the evening, flaunting with life and its desires, trying to hook up with the right man who could take care of her and her children and their needs. If only things had been different then, she thought to herself. If only things could be different now. . . . If only, if only. . . .

Harry had the capability. He'd pulled off a lot of fancy numbers in his day, like the time he had that tip on the Kentucky Derby, borrowed thousands of dollars and took the chance of a lifetime and won that race. They'd lived high on the hog then. But she was afraid. Why, that loan shark would have cut off Harry's arms if he hadn't come back with the money. She'd panicked and paced the floor all night, and when Harry arrived, with that look on his face, she knew that they were dead people. And then that fool started laughing, and she knew he was only playing one of his scams on her. They partied all that weekend, and from that little fiasco she knew she could trust Harry.

He didn't have to treat her and the whole crew to that lavish party at Caesar's Palace. They were living large then, her sister and her. Maybe that's why she was dead now. Diane wanted to live large every day, night and day, and that's what killed her. She ran around with the wrong crowd, and that's what brought her down. All that stealing and scamming and the use and abuse on her body from those high-rollers from all over the country. And they killed her. She knew too much, she talked too much. Her dear baby sister dead at a young age. She had her own compulsive behavior to be with more and more men, wanted more money, more excitement. Well, she finally met her match, and that compulsiveness is what killed her.

It was about time for her to freshen up their drinks. While she did, she'd find out just what the hell Harry was really up to. Why, Benny and Sammy weren't allowed within a hundred miles of the Vegas area, so it had to be something really big, or they would never have taken the risk in coming here.

Benny knew those dice like the back of his hands. He used to trade off in the casinos and was able to stay in the field at $500 a shot for at least an hour. When those casino managers got suspicious, he'd bail out of the game. He was notorious for getting over on those casinos. But that was then and this was now. She wondered what Harry had in store for him and Sammy.

Sammy was the card man in those days. He could place another card into a deck without the dealer ever suspecting him. Sammy would bet heavy and win thousands of dollars a night.

So why were those two here with Harry when they could make their own money? Something big must be going to happen.

7

"Say, fellows," Paula said as she breezed in, "can I freshen up your drinks?"

"Sure, Paula. Come on in and have a seat. I have my own personal stash right here," said Harry. "I was just going over some logistics with Sammy and Benny on Operation Parlay. They both know that you're in with us and will be acting as a confederate."

"Yes," Paula said as she looked around the cigar-smoke-filled room. "Just like the old days, huh, fellows?"

"It's not the same, Paula. Harry is not Sidney Poitier, and this is not the movie, *Sneakers*. In other words, now we're looking at some big time," said Benny. "In the past, all they'd do was run you out of town for a scam like this if you could pull it off. But today, with all of the Fortune 500 corporations investing in Las Vegas, if we pull something off with this magnitude, we're looking at a life sentence if we're caught."

"You can say that again, Benny," said Paula, as she paused and took a quick glance at Harry, now nervous and tense that his old buddies wouldn't go in with him on the heist of the century. Paula had to think and think fast; there had been many times when she pulled Harry out of a jam but this would be the last, she thought to herself as she continued to fix Benny and Sammy their favorite drinks.

"Look at it now, Benny, this is not Las Vegas. Why,

even Bugsy Siegal is turning over in his grave now at all this corporate corruption—that's one thing the founding father of the City of Sin would never permit, and that's bringing in 'KIDS' so the house can collect a fast buck at the casinos."

"Yeah, I guess you do have a point, Paula. Why, I was just reading in the paper how they plan on building the MGM mega-casino with displays of *The Wizard of Oz*; Dorothy carrying Toto and those three characters, the Tin Man, the Scarecrow and the Cowardly Lion on display right in the center of this giant mega-buck casino where the children can grab their parents' hands and tell them that they want to go on the rides and play the video games. Those parents will only ease off and leave those children right there inside the casino while they risk their whole life savings gambling. You're right, Paula; this is not the Las Vegas that we once knew. They're using our children for their own personal gains," Benny said, as he took a stiff drink, turning his glass bottoms up and then passing it back to Paula for a refill.

Harry observed everything slowly and silently and now it was time that he used the old "pitch and close" method to complete the deal.

"Those poor little orphan children, well, that's where they will be, right down there at the St. Vincent Homeless Center after their parents leave them, abandon them right there in those filthy-minded casinos. Don't those corporate executives have any morals and ethics—don't they see what the hell they're doing to the last little values we got left—that's our memory, our fondest memory of Little Dorothy in *The Wizard of Oz*, and how her Auntie loved her so much, and that tornado came along, scooped poor little Dorothy up and blew her away to the twilight zone."

Harry, now taking his handkerchief out of his pocket and wiping his eyes, turned away and seemingly blew his nose.

"I loved that story," Sammy said, crying and openly weeping at just the thought of those corporate casino bosses using little Dorothy as if they were the big tornado scooping her up into a world of gambling and corruption by using all of those subliminal techniques.

"And look what they did to the Excaliber and Lexor Hotel and Casino—using Merlin the 'Musician' to place a spell on the children so that those little darlings can ask their parents for a fortune to play those Circus games while the parents gamble the kids' college funds away in the blink of an eye," Sammy said, now standing up as if he wanted to go "toe to toe" with all those corporate executives that devised this subliminal, scheme-miss subversive plan that now traps the youth to gambling and corruption.

"That's Merlin the Magician, not 'Musician.'"

Harry, knowing that he had them where he wanted them now, for it was not only the money that they would receive, if all things went well, it was the symbol that the City of Sin portrayed and the fact that the one thing that the worst and most corrupt thieves in the world would not tolerate, and that is the abuse and misuse of our children using all those subliminal devices that people could not see or even hear but existed at the casinos from the time that you walked inside until the time that you left, after losing a fortune and your family.

"Well, now all of you know what we're up against, who's in and who's out," Harry said, as Paula was the first one to say that she was absolutely in and raised her hand straight up as if she were saluting Old Glory, the American flag and what it stood for, justice for all. Sammy and the others pledged to the allegiance but Benny was still skeptical.

"I just don't know, Harry, I got to go over the plan one more time before I commit myself," Benny said, while puffing on his cigar.

"Benny, Benny, Benny," said Sammy, "you've never backed out of a deal with old Harry before, so what's with you? How about that farm you wanted? Do you think you can get that kind of money working at your local Seven-Eleven? Come on, Benny. You know damn well you'll never be able to gamble in Jersey, and you have to disguise yourself here in Vegas. So let's hear the rest of the plan in detail. Come on out with it, Harry."

"Okay, here we are at the Golden Nugget, where there's a whole new crew. You won't be recognized, Benny. We can come out of there with at least $35,000 in one night. The casino manager is fairly new, one of the old boys from Jersey's son who needed a job. You should be clear from two A.M. until six P.M. The most unique thing about the Nugget, Benny, is that they went back to the old dice, the ones we used over twelve years ago, and they purchased them from a manufacturer in New York. I had all of this checked out, but they won't sell me any dice. Luckily we have our own stash, ain't that right, Benny?" Harry said, twisting his mustache.

"Sure, Harry. But I want to make certain before I place a $500 field bet with bogus dice. My dice have all sixes on all sides, all right, and unless they changed the game of dice in the last twenty years, the sky's the limit on how much we can win before we're detected."

Harry smiled. "Sammy, you'll work over in the Fremont. They still use only one deck of cards, and it'll be easy for you to double-down dirty by slipping in a deuce when you got a nine up and a ten down in the dumps. You have your old cards from the Fremont, don't you?"

"Yeah, Harry, but I'm not as fast as I was a few years ago. Arthritis has set in on my hands and fingers."

"Well," responded Harry, "you better let Mr. Arthur Ritis sit in on your hand another time, because you got to be quick. Those new dealers got good eyes nowadays, probably from all that baby formula mothers used years ago. They're as sharp as a double-edged blade, and you won't know that you're bleeding until the next morning when you look in the mirror, the mirror of a jail cell if you're caught. So be careful."

"Create one of those optical illusions just like in the old days, Sammy. Wear one of those large diamond rings that reflect off the chandeliers," said Benny as he took another puff on his Cuban cigar.

"This is how it's laid out, fellows, at least the preliminary plans," Harry began.

"All you want to gross is $125,000? You don't need us to do that. You could have called some local boys for that," Benny said.

"No, I just said that's part of the preliminary plans. Now here's the whole shot in a nutshell." Harry turned down the lights and pushed an automatic button as Paula, Benny and Sammy watched a screen come down and the slide projector flash on in the smoky game room. The light from the projector divided the smoke like a conference table would divide a Republican and a Democrat as the four watched the screen, and Operation Parlay's details became known.

"We need the $125,000 to purchase this computer and software programs." The slide showed a Cyclotron FM7000, a Russian computer that was previously designed to get the precise calculations to manufacture atomic bombs and to guide nuclear submarines.

"Come on, Harry, you've gone a little too far with all of this. Now you plan on blowing up the whole world?" said Sammy.

"What the hell do you have here, Harry? You planning on building an atomic weapon?" asked Benny.

"No, no, let's not jump to conclusions, fellows. This computer also has the most advanced capabilities to get into banking and commerce information at the touch of a button anywhere in the world. You know what that means. We'll be able to transfer and receive funds from all over the world!"

"You mean to tell me," said Benny, "that you want to pull off a $125,000 scam at the Fremont and the Golden Nugget just to transfer it somewhere?"

"No, just be patient and feast your eyes on this next slide."

"Harry, is that you? What the hell are you doing with that turban on your head?"

"Yeah, have you flipped or do you plan on blowing up the Arabs or the Saudis?" asked Sammy and Benny.

"No, that's not me, but it could very well be. This slide is of the Prince of Armani, the ruler of one of the richest countries of the Saudi empire. In just a few weeks he'll be right here in Las Vegas, Nevada, gambling off the family fortune."

"Yeah, I remember reading a few things about that rich sheik, Prince Armani from Kafanni," said Sammy. "He blew over twenty million dollars last time he was here in Las Vegas and had to go back home and explain where the money was that those rich Republicans in Washington, D.C., gave him to land those Stealth bombers in his country during the Gulf War crisis."

"He caught hell, all right," said Harry. "But those Republicans covered his ass on that guns-for-hostages move, and now he's going to be here in Las Vegas to collect a few more million dollars. Or, at least the way I have it figured out, those boys in D.C. will get the guillotine by their constituents. The prince plans on talking to the Senate Arms Committee unless those boys squeeze his palms with fifteen million dollars or more."

"So tell me, Harry, where does that advanced Soviet computer fit into all of this? I don't want to sound ignorant, but I don't get it."

"Here's the whole layout on this overhead projector, from A to Z. First, we stake out the Fremont, the Golden Nugget and the Union Plaza Hotel. We check out everything from the lighting, the hidden cameras, who's on duty, especially the casino manager, and take a quick look at the slot machine keyholes, the blackjack tables and the dice tables, especially their positioning and lighting. We heist $60,000 in one night from each casino, each of you working in a different casino."

"Wait a minute, Harry. Who's going to pull off the Union Plaza scam? I thought you said that we were going to be strictly blackjack and dice hits?"

"Oh, I contacted Freddy Francisco to be our slot machine man."

"Oh no! He almost got me twenty years the last time we pulled off a scam," Sammy said. "Count me out. I won't work with that guy."

"How about you, Benny? Is Freddy in or out?"

"Well, I don't know. After all, he did marry my daughter, but that didn't last long. I thought the guy was a little shaky, but he turned out to be okay, although my little girl was disappointed. I got to have him checked out again thoroughly, Harry. After all, he just disappeared out of the game. Word is that he turned informant."

"Well, I guess you'll always be working at that little

hardware store in upper New Jersey, Sammy. Tell the family hello for me. I'll have Harold give you a ride to the airport," Harry said. "It's too bad you're going to be missing out on the two-and-a-half-million-dollar payoff."

"Two and a half million? That's my cut, Harry?"

"Yep. These are inflationary times, and we got to go for the gusto. Now, are you in or out?"

"Count me in. I been waiting for something like this all my life. I'm in," said Sammy.

"Good. Now, let's get back to the plan, and this time please don't interrupt me. Freddy, as you know, is the best key man in the business. He can put some putty into a slot machine keyhole, put in the catalyst so the putty can harden, and make the perfect workable key in a matter of seconds. He'll arrange the computer chip so Paula can get a Mega-Buck payoff, and with that money we'll purchase equipment, like limousines, hire the dancing girls—make ourselves look like a rich sheik and princes and princesses."

"Wait a minute. Now I get it, Harry. You're going to disguise yourself as the rich sheik, make off with his big payoff, and then transfer the money from his winnings into your account!"

"Boy, you're a good student, Benny," Harry chuckled as he used the pointer to show the amount of $60,000 in winnings from each casino. "It's getting late, and I want to have one more meeting when Freddy gets here, so I'll have Harold take you two back to your hotel. Are there any questions?"

"I have a question," said Paula. "How much is my cut?"

"Well, sister-in-law, we'll discuss that tonight. But don't you worry your pretty little head. You'll be paid well. Have a good night's sleep, and I'll call you two guys in the morning." Harry told them he'd be waiting for them at the front entrance.

As Paula fanned at the smoke in the room, she turned to Harry. "You never did answer my question. What am I going to get out of being one of your patsies?"

"Well, Paula, that all depends on you. If everything goes like clockwork, according to plan, you'll gross something in the neighborhood of $175,000," said Harry.

"You mean to tell me that you're going to get over twenty million dollars out of this deal, and all I'm receiving is $175,000?"

"Look, Paula, we have to spend over five million on supplies and equipment. How else am I going to pose as a rich prince?"

"Rich prince. Operation Parlay. This is a bit too much for me, Harry. I don't know where you come up with these scams, but this one beats all. Your parlay is being played out by the people. You're using people like chips on a roulette table throwing them against the wall like dice. There you go, bumping people's heads against the wall like cubical playthings for your own enjoyment and pleasure until you score your point. And that point, your point, is reaching your own threshold—getting off on your compulsive trickery and conniving and scheming. This is the grand parlay, the betting of more than one play, the play to see if we all get away or if we'll all go directly to jail. Your parlay is selfishness and compulsiveness to win big so you can brag about it amongst your gangster friends, while we all sit inside a jail cell!"

"Well, Paula, what you can do is go back to the bottom, to North Las Vegas. You'll be facing greater insurmountable odds there and maybe even have Harold subjected to being murdered right there on that corner where he dealt drugs for half of his childhood. Sylvia will be subjected to being a penny-ante prostitute, selling her body just for a drag on that cocaine pipe. And you—you'll more than likely go back to your lovers, those slot machines. That is, if you can get back on the county welfare system and draw a check every month. Those are big ifs, Paula. But my plan is foolproof, or I wouldn't even attempt it. Why live a life of misery every day and every hour of your life, when you can just take one chance in a lifetime with me?"

"Well, Harry, you've done it again. You've baited me in on that hook of a scam, letting me see part of the good life. You've fed me caviar and champagne, and now you want to throw me back into the ocean, back to North Las Vegas, where the sharks will surely eat me and the kids and then spit us out like garbage. What choice do I have but to go along with your Operation Parlay. You give me no choice whatsoever."

"I'm glad you see it my way, or I should say, our way, because we're in this together," said Harry.

The two retreated to their separate rooms with hope and the element of fear of not only pulling off Operation Parlay, but of waking up tomorrow to face another day.

8

That morning the sun peeked out early, with the temperature already at eighty-two degrees. Sylvia and the baby sat by the poolside, listening to the radio in the backyard full of beautiful roses and immaculate shrubbery and hedges. Sylvia kept hearing a voice singing from the other side of the fence as she listened to the radio and felt as if someone was peering over at her.

She called to the face she saw. "Excuse me, do you have any business over here in my yard?"

"Your yard? I thought Mr. Simmons lived here," said the teenage boy from across the fence.

"Well, I am Ms. Simmons, and I live here now, so please stop watching me sunbathe and stop singing those awful songs."

"I didn't know that Mr. Simmons got married again, and to such a beautiful young wife."

"Harry is my uncle, not my husband, if it's any business of yours. Who are you in the first place?"

"My name is Thomas, Thomas Prescott, and I live here. And what is your name?"

"Sylvia Simmons, and I just moved here. Now, neighbor, can I get some rest, please?"

"You shouldn't be trying to rest with that baby roaming around the pool. Don't you know she might slip into the pool and drown?"

"Well, do you want to watch her?" said Sylvia.

"Sure, that is, if I can come over and swim with you."

"Well, you can come over, but I can't swim. I never learned how."

"You just wait right there while I go back into the house and slip into my swimsuit. I'll give you your fist lesson."

"My first lesson on what?" asked Sylvia in a disconcerted voice.

"Your first lesson in swimming. You see, I'm a certified lifeguard. I work at Wet and Wild water park. I can teach you how to swim."

"Okay, come on over," Sylvia said. "Get your swimming pants on and come on over."

"They're called swimming trunks, and they're somewhat revealing."

"It doesn't matter what the label says, you can still come over."

Thomas ran and put on his tight and most revealing trunks. As he jumped over the fence, Sylvia's mouth dropped wide open as she viewed the well-built young man with muscles from the tip of the toes to his earlobes.

"Wow, you must be a body builder," she said.

"No, I just swim a lot. I'm like a fish when it comes to being in the water."

"Well, do you go upstream to spawn, or do you stay in shallow water?" Sylvia asked sarcastically.

"What are we waiting for? Let's get in." Thomas dove into the Olympic-sized pool and popped up in a flash. Sylvia stood up and walked down to the shallow end. As she walked, she flaunted her body, modeling her new bathing suit that she'd just purchased at Caesar's Mall.

What a body! Thomas thought to himself. Damn, she's got all the right curves in all the right places. As he observed her, she did a Dorothy Lamour performance at the shallow end of the pool, placing her toes in first, and then slipping one foot in at a time, posing and placing her arms on her hips. Thomas felt that he had to do something to stay in the pool, due to the enlargement of his penis. He was physically getting excited as he looked at Sylvia and her fine, fine body.

It's a wonder what good living conditions can do, Sylvia thought. Just look at me now. Once a prune figure while I was on those drugs and running the streets all night, and now I have a body like Christie Brinkley.

Tom splashed water all over Sylvia, and she shook and yelled at Tom, calling him a little punk. Then she kicked water back at him. She lost her balance and began to descend into the water, right into Tom's arms.

A feeling came over the two of them, and love called both of them from the time their eyes met. The blue water of the swimming pool reflected into Tom's blue eyes and reflected off of Sylvia's brown eyes. Thomas gave Sylvia more than a lesson in swimming. He held her like no other man had ever held her, nice and gentle, and showed her how to stroke her arms and paddle her feet in the water. It was like a dream come true for Sylvia, and Thomas enjoyed himself immensely.

"Do you want the baby to learn how to swim?"

"She's too little to swim, isn't she?" said Sylvia.

"No, this is the best time, while she's little and not afraid of the water," Thomas insisted. "You go practice your kicks, Sylvia, while I train the baby."

As Thomas walked to the shallow end of the pool, Sylvia watched the mass of muscle and legs that could match that of the running back, Eric Dickerson, with so much muscle that she could see the development. Sylvia's heart started pounding because of Thomas's kind-hearted gentleness. Why, he even liked the baby. She watched as he gently played with the baby in the water. Little Charlene was enjoying herself. What a difference a day makes, thought Sylvia.

By then, her mother and Uncle Harry had awakened from a restless night and were having breakfast in the kitchen nook. "Well, I see Sylvia is adjusting well to her new environment, Paula," said Harry.

"Yes, it looks that way. Isn't that the young boy from next door whose father is a surgeon?"

"Yes, that's Devereaux Prescott's son. We've been neighbors and good friends for years."

"The way those two are carrying on, it looks like you'll be more than good friends. You may be in-laws. Look at them. They're like two swans in a pond, swimming with each other. I didn't know that Sylvia could even swim. She looks like she's in love—love at first sight."

"Who's that out there with my sister?" Harold asked as he rubbed his sleepy eyes.

"That's the boy from next door, Harold. He's teaching our Sylvia how to swim."

"Sylvia never learned how to swim when I used to try to teach her. This guy must have something really going for himself to be able to stand Sylvia. You know how she gets, Mama, especially with strangers."

"Yes, I know. This is very unusual for her, to be so patient and learn how to swim in such a short period of time. Why, they've only been out there for an hour," Paula said.

"Mama, it must be love," grinned Harold.

"Must be. Maybe this will keep Sylvia's mind off those drugs. Maybe this new fellow will be able to control her compulsive substance abuse habits."

"I doubt it, Mama. Like mother, like daughter. And you know you haven't controlled your habits."

"What do you mean, Harold?"

"Well, the cook told me when you both went to the market the other day he had to wait for two hours until you got off the slot machine there. The food was about to spoil, and the only reason you left that slot machine was because you ran out of money."

"That was my own personal money, Harold, and I can do what I want with it, if you don't mind."

"Mom, you and Sylvia are so much alike. Both of you have the same compulsive behavior. The only difference is that one of you is on drugs while the other one is on slots."

Paula indignantly retorted, "So where were you last night until the wee hours of the morning? You must have driven over to North Las Vegas and dealt some drugs or made arrangements to get some. You know I won't have no drugs around me in this house, so you better get rid of them immediately!"

"No, I didn't buy any drugs. All I did was visit my son and his mother. But I can always tell when you and Sylvia have done something wrong. When Sylvia has smoked drugs, her eyes are as big as the bottom of a Coke bottle and she's always looking down at the ground like she's dropped something—maybe some of that rock cocaine. And you, Mama, are the same way. You look down on the ground every time you lose a whole lot of money, as if you're going to get lucky and find out where some of that money has rolled to. You and Sylvia have the same sickness—greed."

"You go to your room right now, Harold!" Paula demanded. "On second thought, you better go outside and see what your sister is doing with Dr. Feelgood's son. We don't want to come up with another baby, do we?"

"You got that right, Mama. But if Sylvia hooks up with the doctor's son, at least the baby will have some good genes, and not drug junkie genes."

"Boy, you get your ass outside right this minute!"

Harold went through the French double glass doors to meet Thomas. He admired his physique and liked his friendliness and felt instinctively that Thomas was the right person for his sister.

Inside the kitchen, Paula said, "Harry, this Sheik of Armani sure does look like you. Just look at him. The only difference is those cheekbones and that three-day beard. Why, if my husband were alive, I'd swear he was trying to pull a fast one on me. But I know damn well he's dead."

"Let me see that paper. Oh no! The sheik is due here in just one week! I better call Benny, Freddy and the other members of Operation Parlay. We got to get rolling tonight! Paula, call the Union Plaza Hotel and ask for Benny Benniola while I slip into some clothes. Tell him I want the three of them to meet me in the lobby at two o'clock. We got to start Operation Parlay immediately!"

"But, Harry, tomorrow is Harold's birthday, and I want to get him a cake and have a few friends over, if it's okay with you."

"I'll take care of Harold, Paula. But we'll be busy getting the costumes, the Arabian girls, the limos...you know, the works. Just let me handle Harold's birthday party. Tomorrow we go into full operation—Operation Parlay."

9

The stage was set and the players were ready for action as Harold drove Harry to the Union Plaza Hotel to meet with Benny Benniola, the dice man, Sammy Tricoli, the professional artist at the game of blackjack and illusion, and the unexpected and unpredictable Freddy Francisco, the master of the slot machine heist. They would meet in Benny's suite at the Union Plaza Hotel to go over the plans with Freddy and Sammy, but Harold would remain in the lobby near the gift shop and report any unusual circumstances, as he saw it, due to the gathering of the most professional outcasts of crossroaders ever to assemble in Las Vegas, Nevada.

"Now, Harold, you know what to do and how to send a signal up to Benny's room."

"Yes, Uncle Harry."

"Just hang out here and play a few slots and blend in with the crowd. And try not to win anything," Harry laughed.

"Gotcha, Uncle Harry."

Harry passed by the registration desk and the gift shop on his way to the elevator and noticed as he glanced at the main entrance that John Jr.'s Corvette was not parked in its usual place, so the owner was not present. But Harry knew if John Jr. even spotted him near the casino, all the red lights would go off, and that would be the end of Operation Parlay and all those years of training in computer science at UNLV would have been in vain. Harry silently prayed, just let me get to the twelfth floor and go over the "main menu" with all three of them to make sure that there will be no mistakes.

This new diagonal carpet that John Junior installed is making me dizzy, Harry thought. Why, it is drawing me back to the tables, those poker tables that I almost lost a fortune and my fourth wife gambling all night—just look at those aces with diagonal arrows pointing to the poker tables, but the reverse of those diagonal cards is on this new carpet . . . the cards are folded down as if I want to lift them up and take a peek of what the next card is going to be. It's giving me the shakes, just like a junkie hooked on drugs, inticing me to play again and win; take a chance, what do I have to lose? That alcohol, it's reacting with those patterns on the carpet bringing me in closer and closer, back to the poker tables—I got to be strong or I will risk a chance of a lifetime—it's either twenty million or the poker table for an instant gratification—damn this subliminal shit is strong; you can't see it, you can't feel it, and it is only a threshold reaction of your past experience of winning or getting a maximum peak experience. Come on elevator, hurry it up before all these subliminal signals lure me back in to the devils' dungeon where time stands still . . . oh God, thank God . . . the elevator is here and I am saved, going straight up toward heaven. . . .

As Harry knocked on the door of room 1205, chills went down his spine. He thought, there is big, big money involved in this one, and that's the only reason that I'm getting these butterflies. He was concerned about his niece, nephew, and his sister-in-law. Things had to go right, they just had to.

Benny let Harry in. Harry walked straight over to the wet bar and fixed himself a triple-Seven and told the three,

"This triple-Seven is for you fellows and your newfound fortune! You know the routine; Freddy, Benny, and Sammy have clued you in to what is in it for you. But the only hitch is that we have to work fast now, and move our hardware to the Strip, where we go into operation. Freddy, do you have your key kit?"

"Yeah, Harry."

"So what we'll do is work in a triangle, hitting three casinos all at the same time and then rotating, since we'll have less risk in being caught and called in when or if we're discovered. When we've reached our $125,000 limit, we'll put the show on the road at the Mirage, Caesar's, and the Tropicana. Everybody's take will be $65,000 apiece. We'll meet at Caesar's . . . you all know the room number. We're from the old school, and it'll be just like the old days. Now, let's get busy. Oh, and one other thing. Sylvia, my niece, will be working as a confederate, along with Paula and Harold, so if you get in a jam, just look over your shoulder and they'll create a getaway-with-the-goodies scene. Is all of this understood, fellows?"

"Yeah, Harry, it's a piece of cake. But how about you? How are we going to get the computer and other equipment here on time before the Sheik gets here?" asked Freddy.

"Don't worry, I have everything covered. Just meet us at Caesar's at around six A.M., and make sure everybody comes up with their fair share. One other reminder, rotate and don't get caught in the same club at the same time. Is that understood?"

"Sure, Harry. See you at six A.M."

Harry concluded the conference, making his point short and sweet, then walked out of the room, making certain he'd put a bug in the ears of all three men that they were going to be watched by Paula, Sylvia and Harold. Harry had no intention whatsoever of letting his three safeguards know about any of the initial hits on the casinos.

In the lobby, Harry looked for Harold, but couldn't find him. Where was that boy? He scanned the slot machines, then looked over at the sports betting section. That kid had to pay more attention to detail. Harry knew if they saw him in here, he was a dead man.

He saw Joe, the cab driver, at the bar. He tried to hide from him, knowing he'd ask him a favor, so turned toward the sports betting section to hide, then he could escape out the side door in the valet parking section where Harold had parked the car. If Harold blew this thing after all his hard work, he'd kill him.

The sports betting must have been remodeled, and it looked like they had a new crew. That was good, he wouldn't be recognized. There was a new man working behind the cage. In all his years in Las Vegas, this was the first time he'd ever seen an Afro-American working in the sports-betting section. There must have been an inquiry about having more Afro-Americans in higher management. The only other Afro-American working in the whole Las Vegas area in a high profile position was at the Hilton, and there were bets all over town that he wouldn't last a year. Well, maybe things were getting better for some minorities here in Las Vegas. Maybe one day he'd see an Afro-American casino owner . . . maybe, one day.

They had laid new carpet and installed overhead TV monitors at the racetrack betting. This place sure had changed. He placed a sports paper in front of him so he wouldn't be noticed. There was some commotion over in a corner, and some runners were arguing over a bet that a new guy must have placed into the computer. Those guys would never learn. Runners were always betting a thousand dollars a play, and the only reason was to launder some dirty money from the East Coast. They were trying to give the new kid a hard time, arguing with him. After the smoke cleared, he'd go up to the counter and place a small wager just to say a few words to the new guy, give him some encouragement and let him know that he was dealing with scum.

"Give me a dime on 6034, 6037, 6039, and 6040," said Harry as he reached for his money clip to pay for the $1,000 parlay of bets.

"Sir, that's ten ten-dollar bets on a parlay of 6034...."

"No," said Harry. "A dime is a bet of a thousand dollars here in Las Vegas. Son, you got to learn the language before knowing the game. How long have you been working here at the Union Plaza Hotel and Casino?"

"This is my first day," said the man, feeling embarrassed, and only trying to do good and be polite.

"Well, who's training you, John? John is your name, right, according to your name tag that you have on upside down."

"Mr. Goodin is training me, sir, and today is my first day ever working in a casino."

"Well, John, if you make mistakes like you just did, it will not only cost you your job, it may cost you your life. So be careful. If you have any questions about sports betting, call me at my house. I'm listed. Harry Simmons is my name."

"Come on before the board goes down!" someone yelled from behind Harry.

"Hold your horses, buddy." Harry looked over his shoulder, and it was none other than Joe, the cab driver.

"Harry, is that you?" Joe asked.

"Yeah, it's me, in the flesh and bone. I thought you gave up sports betting, Joe."

"Oh, I got a tip on a few teams, Harry. But if this one doesn't come through I'll give it up once and for all."

"Yeah, sure, that's what they all say. You take it easy, kid, and take your time. Be sure to call me sometime."

"Yes, Mr. Simmons, I will. And thanks."

"And, kid, don't let these high-rollers like Joe get you nervous. We want to see more of your kind working here in the casino instead of dealing drugs in North Las Vegas. Take it slow."

"Say, Harry, do you need a ride?" asked Joe.

"No thanks, Joe. My nephew is around here somewhere."

"I think I saw him talking to the cocktail waitress right over there, Harry."

"Thanks, Joe."

"Harry, if you need a driver anytime soon, you know how to contact me."

"Yeah, I'll need a driver next week, so be prepared for anything and everything," said Harry cryptically.

"Thanks, Harry. It'll be just like the old days."

"See you next week, Joe."

He had to find Harold and get the hell out of here before someone else saw him in here. The heat would be on by tomorrow after six in the morning.

"Harold, where did you go? You were supposed to be watching out for me. What happened?"

"I was watching your back, Uncle Harry. From the time you got off the elevator and walked through the slot machine area and into the sports betting section, I had you covered."

Harry's mouth dropped open in surprise. Harold was so much like his own twin brother, Harold Senior, and himself. Harold Junior had made the transformation into a true hustler, always having an answer for everything, always making an excuse for the errors and life's little pleasures, always seeing things his own way. It was a genetic time bomb that just needed activating. Harold earned his initiation into the brotherhood of crossroaders from that very moment.

As they drove home, Harry thought to himself, what have I created? Harold's just like his dad and me. Once you're in the game, you're in for life. Now this whole thing is coming full circle. It's that compulsiveness I learned about from attending UNLV, that psychology class that explained how some things are predisposed through nature. Suddenly a person finds out that he has hidden talents, either the gift of gab or the ability to use artistic talents. It's all genetic, if you ask me.

But in his family there was a little gene that gave them the ability to lie, cheat and con everybody to meet their compulsive desires. Now that he'd dealt with people all his life, he understood their needs, sexual and psychological. If he got out of this alive, he might even apply to a program to obtain his Ph.D. in psychology.

"Harold, tonight is your birthday, and we're going to celebrate it at Caesar's Hotel and Casino."

"Great! Are we going to have ice cream and cake?"

"Not this time. I think it's time you grew up. There will be cream, but not cake," Harry chuckled.

Harold's face looked mystified as he drove down the Strip and entered Caesar's valet parking.

"Our room number is 777, Harold. You take the computer key card and go on up, make yourself comfortable, and order me some steak and lobster. I'm going to walk over to the Mirage with my attaché case and scope things out."

"Thanks, Uncle Harry! Oh, can I order champagne?"

"Sure. Tonight's your night. We'll be having guests, so

just let them in and make them comfortable." Harry smiled to himself. That little bastard thinks he's so smart, so grown-up, but after tonight he'll really be a man. He grabbed his attaché case out of the trunk of Harold's Mustang convertible. Harold was just like a child. If you didn't watch him, he'd get burned every time. He could have blown his cover at the Union Plaza, and then Harry would have had to answer to the league of high-rollers. He would have been the laughingstock of the crossroaders, caught with his pants down.

Tonight he was going to turn Harold on to some real women. He was twenty years old now, and it was time he learned how to have a real romance and get rid of those childish puppy love syndromes for those stupid young girls he was used to in North Las Vegas.

Tonight there would be a grand rehearsal for phase two of Operation Parlay. Harold walked from Caesar's Palace to the Mirage Hotel and Casino carrying a typical attaché case. The only difference was that this case had a special concealed camera that could take pictures or slides just by pushing a button on top. Harry had to get pictures of the layout. Hotels and casinos were always redecorating and rearranging things, especially for special guests. There was no room for mistakes on this one. This one had to be foolproof, or someone's ass—probably his—would fry.

The six-foot-two Harry strolled through the Mirage. Ladies of all nationalities gave the debonair and handsome man wearing designer clothing the nod. His walk, his projection of high-class gentry that Harry emanated made his presence fearsome to any male attached to a beautiful female companion. Harry was a cross between Tyrone Power and Cary Grant, and the only thing observably different was his color. He was an Afro-American, but with English features.

He took a shot of the cashier's cage, where the Prince of Armani would sign for his note. He had to know the positioning of the video cameras and where the cashiers would be positioned. Over there were the poker tables. Although the prince didn't play much poker, he might watch one of his people play a little, as he had before. Next he snapped a few shots of the layout of the blackjack, roulette and the dice tables, the Prince's favorite games. A few of the rest room area, just in case his disguise and make-up began to wilt. Last but not least, the exits, just in case he had to make a quick getaway.

Steve Flynn, the owner, couldn't have planned this hotel better. The exits, entrances, and all the false deceptions of the fish aquariums, tigers and dolphins, would play into his hands like a sculptor masterminding a piece of art. The beautiful curves on his model would be the roulette wheel; the hairlines would be like the dice on the crap table, and the mouth of his beautiful model would be like that exit sign, reminding him it was time to get the hell out of there.

He had to get back and call a few people to rehearse this Egyptian illusion and deception. Maybe he could get in touch with the costume factory in Hollywood tonight and tell them to put a rush on those costumes. They only had seven days.

Harry tilted his hat and proceeded through the lobby, steadily taking pictures with the hidden camera, then he proceeded down the escalators and headed towards Caesar's Hotel and Casino.

10

Harold parked the car in the valet parking section and caught the elevator to the seventh floor of Caesar's Hotel and Casino. As he walked, he admired the statues of gladiators and Roman soldiers and the beautiful water fountains and marble pillars. Boy, he thought, if they lived like this back then, I was born in the wrong century. But then, they would probably have fed my kind to the lions, anyway. Black people never had anything in those days, and never would have anything as long as there were white people alive.

As he approached one statue of a Roman soldier Harold noticed that it was a Black man, with strong muscles and a crown. The inscription said that Humanis was once a king in the Egyptian tribe near Cairo, and the pyramids that were built could be attributed to King Humanis and his ancestry from the boy, King Tutankhamen.

Wow! He never knew that. They never taught anything about Black history in his school, and that was a damn shame. Maybe he might have a little more self-esteem and dignity if he'd known that Black people had achieved something in their lives. Not all Blacks were slaves and thieves as the white man depicted. Some Blacks had been important throughout history. He wondered why they didn't teach about Black history in elementary school. Were they afraid, or didn't they know about Blacks in history? The only time he'd learned anything about Black people was during Black history month, and that was the shortest month of the whole year—February!

The elevator was plush, with carpet and mirrors, and as Harold admired himself he began to identify with the statue he'd seen of the Black king. "I could have been a king, maybe." Harold flexed his muscles and posed in the mirror. "I could have been that boy king." But something had happened to his people, he didn't know what. Blacks didn't have shit now. From those statues and pictures, they had once "lived large."

Stepping out of the elevator, he found his room. How could you open a door with a piece of plastic? he wondered to himself. He stood outside the door, mystified over the fact that there was no keyhole, just a plastic slot. Well, they must have taken our Afro-American brains when they put us in slavery, because I don't know how to get inside this damn room.

Just then a man passed by and noticed Harold's difficulty. "What's wrong, son?"

"Oh, this plastic doesn't want to open up this door."

"Let me help you." The gentleman with a German accent helped Harold open the double doors of the suite. "Now you can go in, son. Just place the plastic card in the direction of the arrows, pull it out, and open the door when the green light goes on. That's all there is to it!"

"Thank you, mister," Harold said. He thought to himself, all white people weren't that bad. The way Blacks were in his old neighborhood, with the drive-by shootings and gangs, Afro-American people's ancestors probably sold themselves into slavery for a few pieces of gold, silver, or moonshine; look what's happening now with crack cocaine. White people had their own problems, too. They were just as scared of life. We live all together in this world; maybe we could help each other.

Harold watched the man who'd helped him open the door to his room proceed down the hallway, and then he stepped into paradise. Harold gasped as he opened the double doors to Suite 777, the Roman Palace room. It was three times the size of the roach den they'd lived in in North Las Vegas. A marble jacuzzi with gold fixtures and a wet bar were sunk right in the middle of the floor. This was luxury!

Harold's eyes were huge as he played with all of the amenities, like opening presents on Christmas Day. The wet bar could be raised up and down automatically by touching a button. And there was a fifty-two-inch television he could control right from the jacuzzi!

He was in heaven, and a far cry from North Las Vegas. But what had he died of? he wondered. Probably ignorance. Yeah, not knowing that luxury like this existed. Boy, Uncle Harry must be rich. He wondered why Operation Parlay was so important to him. It seemed to Harold that this was all the parlay anybody could want. If not, Uncle Harry could buy more. This room must cost a thousand dollars a night!

Why couldn't he have something like this in life? He'd tried going to school, but how the hell could you make it in school and then come home and try to study with a nagging mother and a begging sister and a crying crackhead baby? Besides, no schooling bought all of this. This stuff wasn't obtained by getting an education. Sure, maybe the architect went to school, but the people who stayed here for the weekend and lived high made their money some other way. He couldn't see anyone spending a thousand a night for a room, and then come Monday morning going back to work hard for the rest of the week. These rooms were for the high-rollers like Uncle Harry.

He laughed. Hell, the welfare system only gave his

mama seven thousand dollars a year with food stamps, and this room alone cost a thousand a night, not including food and drinks.

Speaking of drinks, he thought he'd fix himself one. After all, it was his birthday. There was no reason to dwell on what he didn't have. He had it all for now.

As Harold went from the main room to the bathroom, he was surprised to see a television and telephone right there that could be used while releasing "unwanted substances." You could watch television or talk on the phone while sitting on the pot or taking a bubble bath! Wow, a double-face bowl and a toilet that flushed itself—either these people were lazy or they were just crazy with comfort!

He was beginning to understand why it was important for Harry to keep money, and lots of it. He'd been used to living like this, and he had to keep on living like this or his dreams would be shattered forever.

The hell with trunks. He was here alone, and the Romans didn't have swimsuits. They just jumped in wearing their birthday suits. And after all, it was his birthday! Harold jumped into the bubbling jacuzzi in the nude. He blasted the jets and sat with the remote in hand, flipping from channel to channel like a flashing neon sign. Colors were bouncing off the walls from the reflection of the television.

The telephone rang several times, but Harold refused to answer it while he was in the jacuzzi; he didn't want his dream interrupted, and he didn't want to leave this Paradise on Earth. This was heaven! This life was too good to be true, and for a nineteen-year-old about to turn twenty, this was the best of life.

He picked up another remote. It read CD—compact disc player, maybe? Harold hit the play button and the sounds of Prince blasted off the walls of the hotel suite. It was like having a symphony orchestra right there in the room with him. All he needed was to freshen up his drink and he'd be good to go.

With drink in his left hand and CD remote in his right, Harold stood butt naked while Prince was jamming the song "Seven" full blast. Suddenly the double doors opened, and his Uncle Harry, along with five beautiful showgirls, entered, wearing not much more than a pure party attitude. Harold attempted to reach for a towel, but the girls said, "Don't worry, honey, we've seen it before."

"We tried to call you from downstairs, but you didn't answer the phone. Now you're caught with your pants down, son, or should I say, no pants on at all. Happy birthday, Harold!" said Uncle Harry. "It's twelve o'clock, so let's party!" Harry retreated to the adjoining suite with two of the showgirls, telling Harold that a special girl named Melinda was changing into her costume and would be right out.

Harold wanted to pinch himself to find out if this was true or if he was dreaming. The lyrics kept going on and so did the drinks. The girls got busy with Harold, all of them in the jacuzzi, getting blasted, not on drugs, but on fantasy.

When Melinda came out, Harold was stunned. She was the finest girl he had ever seen in his life. He figured she must be from Europe, because he'd never seen anything like her around these parts, only on television. She was from India, or perhaps Saudi Arabia, and had an exotic beauty that captivated him.

All the girls were laughing and they seemed to like him, but he knew they were professional call girls, in it for the money. But Melinda was different, and she had his temperature rising fast.

Harry came out of the adjoining suite and asked Harold if everything was okay.

"Uncle Harry, can I talk to you for a minute?"

"Sure, son, what is it?"

"Well, I kind of like Melinda, and the others are sort of in the way...."

"Okay, I'll tell the others that the party is over for them. And, Harold, you better fix your towel. The family jewels are showing."

Harold jumped back into the jacuzzi with Melinda, and the other girls were paid off their share for that evening and walked out through the double doors of the suite.

Sensuous and sexual, that would describe her. Sensational! They must have imported her from a foreign country where women respected the men and never talked back or got smart. She was a dream come true—her lips shaped like a fresh-picked Georgia peach and her eyes as bright as the moon and pure white as the driven snow.

Melinda didn't speak much English, but he was getting her messages as she began to belly dance around the room for him. Round and round those muscles turned, like a Cosby commercial for Jello. He gazed at her perfect beauty, her teeth so straight that his first inclination was that they weren't hers. Whoever her parents were, they had groomed her well, and not for a young city boy like him, he thought. He had nothing to offer this girl of his dreams, and it appeared the only thing she had to offer him was love.

The color of her skin was not black and not brown; it was like a caramel color. With her hair long and dark, she would have no problem being a model. Hmmm, he thought. That's all I could offer her. He'd taken a few classes in photography. Maybe she would gain confidence in him if he offered to help her become a model. It was his only hope of keeping her. He was in love and wanted her to be his.

The music kept repeating, but he didn't want to reach over for the remote control, since he and Melinda were caught in a passionate whirlwind of sensual delight in the jacuzzi. She was touching him all over, and as he kissed her he inhaled the soft fragrance of her long hair. She showed him positions that he didn't know existed as the music wailed out of the CD.

So appropriate were the lyrics at the time of making love, they would be imprinted on his memory forever. From here to eternity it would be just he and Melinda.

*   *   *

While Harold was lost in "life's little pleasures," Benny, Freddy and Sammy were taking care of business, too, at the Union Plaza, the Fremont, and the Golden Nugget Hotels.

"This just isn't my line of work any more," Benny thought out loud as he approached the dice table. "This will be the last time for me." He had to get psyched out and be prepared for the worst and the best. None of the people he'd known in the past were around, so he decided to muzzle in at the craps table and make a trade-off.

There were three people to go before the dice would be in his corner. He'd have less than thirty minutes to hold his phony dice, loaded with sixes, before he might be detected. The dice were coming his way, and for the first time he was clamming up. Maybe it was his age, or maybe his nerves were gone. Maybe he was worried about Harry. Could he really pull this thing off like he said he could . . . ?

Well, Harry was right about one thing for sure, Benny

thought to himself, and that's how these casinos have changed in the past twenty years; they don't pass out any cigars like they used too, just those watered down drinks. I got to survey the area before making my move . . . why, they got cameras all in the ceilings, one camera looking at the players, the other camera watching the other camera and the state of Nevada camera being surveyed by the Federal Internal Revenue camera; this is nuts . . . no one can trust the other; I wonder how and why the feds let places like this stay in business. They even hire outside people to keep up the excitement by yelling when they get a lucky win; that brings in the suckers, Harry said; after all those years of being tricked, thanks to Harry's plan, somebody will finally get these phony penny-ante, profit-taking hustlers back . . . now it's my turn to take the dice. . . .

"Five big ones on the come line and five big ones in the field." The stick man, a young playboy-type with a German accent, looked at Benny and then tried to get the casino manager's approval. But the casino manager was occupied at another table, so the stick man okayed the bet of $1,000.00. Benny threw the dice as far as possible while he switched one die with a phony, six-die cube. The probability of a field bet was 2, 3, 5, 9, 12 as the client on the other end placed the long-lost dice on the table. With Benny's long sleeves, he traded a die off for a bogus die and threw a nine.

"Play that five hundred around the world" said Benny and tossed a twelve, which paid double in the field. The crowd yelled out as Benny kept throwing all field bets and winning. In just a matter of twelve minutes, Benny stayed on the dice and was up to a total of $17,000.00 in winnings. He felt it was time to make another trade-off on the dice before the casino manager came back to the table and checked out the dice. He threw the one die off the table so far and acted like he was intoxicated to the point where he couldn't even find his winnings. Now he would pick up a legal pair of dice and they would never find the one he threw. Benny received a new pair of dice while the stick man watched Benny intently and tried to get the attention of the casino manager.

"Damn it, crapped." Benny had crapped out and began to scrape up the black chips. He wanted to hit the door before he was detected.

"Sir, can we comp you a room and dinner for tonight?" said the stick man. He knew that his job was at stake.

"No thanks, son," said Benny. "I'm on my way to the chapel to get married. All these black chips are gonna make a beautiful gift for my bride," he said, lighting a large cigar and making for the door.

That was close. Never again. He didn't care what the hell Harry said, he was too old for this sort of thing. His heart could go out on him. He must have at least two hundred black hundred-dollar chips, the best he'd ever done in such a short time. He wanted to get off the streets and into the Fremont. He'd have Harry or that dumb-looking nephew of his cash these chips in. He was a dead man if he ever entered that casino again.

That damned Harry! Why did he fall for his gimmicks all the time? wondered Sammy as he sat at the blackjack table. If he got busted, these corporate owners here at the Golden Nugget would send him straight up the river. Luckily, it was early in the morning, and all the old players who might recognize him had gone home. What was the limit at this table—a thousand. What the hell, he'd play $750 a hand so he won't attract the attention of the casino manager.

The female dealer called the casino manager for

approval of the large bet as she dealt the cards. The bet was approved, but the casino manager stayed right there and watched Sammy as the cards were being shuffled. Sammy got nervous and thought maybe he might be detected, but after the casino manager saw Sammy's show card, he felt Sammy didn't have a chance at winning. Sammy was showing a deuce and had a ten buried face down, while the dealer was showing a king and had another king face down.

Sammy asked to double down as he placed another $750 on the table. The dealer yelled out to the manager, "Money plays," and as soon as the dealer dealt the card and turned her head for that brief second, Sammy traded off the card she'd dealt him for a nine, giving him twenty-one and a winning of $3,000.00 for the first shot.

Sammy sensed that the dealer was getting suspicious, but he decided to sit it out for at last two more hands. Then the casino manager looked at Sammy and said, "That ring is beautiful. Is it a whole carat?"

"No," replied Sammy, "it's a carat and a half." The dealer had dealt Sammy a blackjack, and he doubled his winnings one more time and left the table.

He'd better find another casino. It was getting too hot around here. Besides, there was Benny over at the dice table. It was time they rotated.

"Seeing is believing; why, these little slot machines got a damn mind of their own; just listen to those looney tunes, why, they're calling me to play with them and I ain't even put a plug nickel in it. I can't believe it; why, this one is winking at me as if she is seducing me; that queen and king on this here poker video just a-turning their heads back and forth telling me to bet the max . . . yeah, right, I'll show you little peeping toms what is the max . . . the maximum amount of this high-powered drill when I line up a royal flush; you can't fool me you little sly slot machine.... Freddy adjusted the cards by placing a specially made drill bit through the corner of the glass while no one was watching him and then used the drill bit to adjust the wheel on the cards to come out with a royal flush that paid $1500.

"Now look who's smiling, sister," Freddy said, as he walked away from the video poker machine after being paid in full by the attendant.

"I hope this drill bit doesn't make too much noise," Freddy muttered under his breath as he shielded his trench coat around the Mega-Bucks slot machine and drilled a tiny little hole. He would stop the wheel as it spun around by using a thin wire placed inside the hole. He dropped five silver dollars into the slot and pulled the handle. The wheels were spinning. Freddy knew the only way it would pay off was if all of the bars, the cherries, or the watermelons lined up, or at least two of them, and then the one on the right could be controlled by Freddy with the thin baling wire.

One watermelon . . . and now there were two lined up! Now to line up that last one without scratching the wheel with the wire. Then it came.... He got it! JACKPOT! The bells began to ring and people gathered around as Freddy hid his tools and waited for the casino manager to come by and give him a payoff of more than forty-seven thousand dollars.

"Sir, do you mind if we take your picture?" the casino manager asked as he presented Freddy with the check.

"No, please! You see, I'm not supposed to be here. You know, the other woman.... You can put the check in her name...Paula Simmons. Thank you very much. She's waiting outside for me in the car. Thank you," Freddy said, "and goodbye."

He ran out of there like a bat out of hell with the check and decided that he would calm down at the Fremont Hotel and play there for a while, then call it a night. The things he did for Harry! But then, Harry had always bailed him out of a jam, and now he could reciprocate. But after this one, he was finished with it. It took his life away, all this gambling. It was too much anymore. He would retire after this last big hit.

In the last two hours, the three men had made off with more than eighty thousand dollars. They met at the Fremont Hotel to make one more move, then call a cab and go to Caesar's Hotel.

"It's too much wear and tear on me, Sammy. I can't do it like I used to. I've gotten old and lost my nerves," said Benny.

"You're telling me! Why, I almost had a heart attack when that casino manager walked up to me to ask about the diamond ring I was wearing. I'll never wear it again! I was almost recognized."

"That drill and wire ain't going to work no more. Never again for me," Freddy said.

"Look, we got near eighty-seven thousand dollars. Why not call it a night? It's damn near four-thirty, and Harry is probably waiting to hear from us. Let's take a cab to Caesar's," suggested Benny.

"Yeah, our lives ain't worth the risk. This place has changed too much for me. It's run by the machines. That slot machine should have paid triple that amount, but it didn't. Everything is preprogrammed. Computer chip mechanisms and those corporate M.B.A. whiz kids got control of this place. It's no more fun, and it's a waste of time. See you guys at Caesar's," said Freddy as the three left, using separate cabs to be careful so they wouldn't be detected.

At Caesar's, Harold lay on the round bed between silk sheets with the newly found love of his life, Melinda. The two were completely exhausted after a "night of all nights." Harold not only became a man, he blossomed into a gentleman as he released the boyhood fears and gained manhood from a real lady. The transition from boy to man also contained a chemical compound known as true love and affection between the two, something that would always be felt deep down inside the two lovers.

"Those three should be getting back here any time now," Harry said, waking up in the adjoining hotel suite. It was close to 5:30 A.M. He walked to the marble bathroom wearing all-silk pajamas imported directly from the China mainland. When he heard the intercom doorbell, he flicked a switch to respond.

"Harry, it's Freddy," a voice said.

Harry pressed a button and said, "Come on back, Fred. Harold is still asleep. He had a long night, his birthday party night."

Freddy walked back to Harry's suite, stepping over clothes and discarded towels. He couldn't help but notice Harold and Melinda asleep in the nude in the round bed.

"Whew, they must have had a hell of a party," Freddy said as he made his way through the littered room, stepping over champagne bottles, corks and clothes. He turned to Harry. "Buddy, I got some good news and some bad news. We ran into a little trouble," Freddy said nervously, "and. . . . "

"And what? You guys got the take, didn't you?" Harry said without hesitation.

"Sure, Harry, but not all of it." Freddy tossed a night drop bag on the bed as Harry wiped his face with a wet towel.

"So what's the problem? And where are Benny and Sammy?"

"Oh, they're both downstairs having breakfast. Here's the bad news. We could only get $87,000, and we barely got that."

"What?! Freddy, you know this operation is too critical for anybody to come up short. What the hell are Sammy and Benny doing downstairs? You know damn well that they could be recognized. You get down there and get them while I get dressed, and then I'll once again show you three how it's done—the right way, the first time around."

Freddy left in a panic as Harry opened the safe in the closet and placed the bag inside. As the door closed, he thought to himself, I'd better check the contents first. He gasped in shock. Those idiots! They had accepted a check, and it was in Paula's name! Didn't they know a check from the casino could be traced back to him! Or at least to Paula when she cashed it.

He knew he had to wake up Harold so he could drive him home to get Paula to cash the check. They were way behind schedule. Those three were just like little children. You had to watch them and hold their hands every time they went out to play.

Harry called Harold on the intercom system and told him to get ready. Waking up next to Melinda's warm body, Harold caressed her and they curled into a little ball.

"Harold, can you hear me? Get ready! We got to make a few runs."

Harold could barely open his eyes. He found the intercom switch and responded by telling Harry that he had a hangover and to catch a cab.

"Why that little bastard!" Harry said angrily. "This is

the last time I'll introduce him to any women!" It was obvious if he wanted anything done right, he'd have to do it himself, he thought as he got dressed. Why, he could have done this whole thing by himself. Timing was critical, and the clock was steadily ticking.

The three arrived at the room and Harry outlined the contingency plan. "Guys, I got to come up with something like forty thousand dollars by one o'clock today, or the whole game is finished. Here's what we'll do. The mail drop at the Mirage is at eleven o'clock at the hotel reservation counter. I'll carry this bag that opens at the bottom by this lever, place it over the mailbag and take the mail. There have to be a few checks in the morning mail. All I want you to do is create a distraction so I can make my move. There's a rest room down the hall from the fish aquarium where I can go through the mailbag and then return it to the counter top. Can you guys do that?"

"What's that, Harry?"

"Create a distraction, an illusion, Sammy. You know, the same thing you do with those cards. The same thing David Copperfield does. Just be a magic man for a few minutes." Harry was frustrated at the three as they all proceeded downstairs with the trick bag. "When you three come back to the room after I've made my move, use the other door. Harold is still asleep. Come on, I've got to catch a cab home and get my check forgery tools."

Either those three had become senile or they were just stupid, Harry thought as he stepped on the escalator, leaving the three and proceeding to the Mirage Hotel and Casino. He had to have that $125,000 before one o'clock. That computer would be arriving by UPS at that time, and it was a C.O.D. deal.

Good help was getting harder and harder to find. First

he got Harold a girl, and now he was still in bed with her. When he got back to the house, he'd have to explain to his mother where he was. He knew he'd catch hell, and on top of that have to listen to her big mouth.

She was too protective of that boy. After his brother had died, Harry had asked her for Harold, but she'd called Harry every name in the book just because he was in the hustling game. She thought he'd be a negative influence on the boy. Ha, and there he was a few months ago dealing drugs on the street corner.

At the registration counter at the Mirage he looked around appreciatively. That young buck, Steve Flynn, sure enough designed a hell of a casino here, he thought. Flynn knew how to bait them, with those tigers and fish and volcanoes erupting. People were bound to drop a few coins in the slot machines just for the environment.

Well, after this caper, he would be far away from all of these commercial casino contraptions, living on his tobacco farm in Venezuela. He was old enough to receive his Social Security, and he sure couldn't live off that little check here in the City of Sin. He had two hundred acres staked out down there. That would be his retirement income, growing tobacco and selling it to Phillip Morris.

Here came the mail drop. Where the hell were those three idiots? He had to get to that mail before the girl at the desk picked it up. Oh, my God! Freddy was inside the fish aquarium, swimming with the baby sharks! People were running from all over the casino just to see the fool.

It was the diversion he needed. Harry placed the trick bag over the mail package, got the mail and got the hell out of there. He hurried to the rest room, where he took a few payroll checks from the accounting firm of Payne, Leibert and Myers. They must be the accountants for the

Mirage. This was his lucky day! All the payroll checks were there! This would net him the amount he needed, and a lot more.

Next he would put the mailbag back where he got it before they got suspicious. They wouldn't realize their checks were missing until that afternoon, and by then he'd get Sylvia to cash a few of them to make up for the money the three stooges hadn't come up with.

Security had Freddy and they were taking him in. Oh boy, now he'd have to bail the fool out of jail. If it wasn't one thing, it was another. Right now, though, he had to catch a cab home and make up some identification for Sylvia so she could cash these checks. He had to meet the one o'clock deadline or Operation Parlay would be ruined.

11

Harry, the King of the Crossroaders, always managed to keep himself out of jail, Paula thought to herself as she sipped her coffee in the kitchen of the Simmons' estate. She wondered what her husband would be doing now if he were still alive. Those two were identical twins, both intelligent, but Harry was always in the hustling game, while Harold, her husband, was more of a skirt chaser. Both of those fools had been really something in their day, and good-looking wasn't the word for it. In Atlanta, they were the talk of the town, and all the women wanted to get with them, either one of them.

But she got what she wanted, and that was Harold, Senior. Too bad things didn't work out. She had two of his children and then found out that he had several spread all the way from the bottom of the Mississippi to the top of that old river.

Speaking of old, here came Harry now. She wondered where Harold Junior was. Oh Lord, she hoped Harry hadn't got Harold involved in some hustling mess.

Operation Parlay, Harry was telling those two stoolies the other night. Why couldn't they just get a job like normal people and be with their families? They were all sick individuals and should probably check into Charter Hospital. Harry was all wrapped up in this Operation Parlay, like some general in the army on a mission. Didn't he know that a parlay is a gamble of the winnings

115

that one had? That was probably the old boy's plan from the beginning.

He was planning to parlay us, she thought. We are his. He gives us all this luxury, and if we don't do things his way, he'll set us on the curve back to the dumps. His family must have been former slave masters the way he plays us and tries to trade us off. Well, if he's put any harm to my Harold, I'll shove that parlay straight up his. . . .

"Paula," Harry called, "I'm back."

"Back from where, Harry, and where is Harold?"

"Harold's fine, Paula. He's with a lady friend, celebrating his birthday."

"Celebrating his birthday? Celebrating his birthday? Where and how long will he be celebrating? All year?"

"Look Paula, like I told you years back, let that boy do his own thing and stop pampering him. He's a grown man now, and if you'd listened to me years ago, he'd have been better off today."

"What do you mean, better off? If he had been with you, he'd probably be dead today, like his father. Yeah, Harry, I know that the Mob was after you that night when Harold Senior got killed. They mistook Harold for you. They wanted you, Harry, with all of your hustling and conniving up in Jersey. They killed Harold, my husband, but they were really looking for you, Harry."

"Oh, shit, here we go again. Listen, Paula, I told you years ago that isn't how it happened. I'd never jeopardize my other half. Harold was my brother, and I loved him. He was my other half, my twin. So stop trying to put the blame on me."

"We baked a cake for Harold Junior for his birthday, and he never showed up. What did you do with my son?"

"Harold's at Caesar's Hotel with a girl he just met. Look, Paula, he's a man, so stop treating him like a two-

116

year-old. How do you expect him to mature if you're always pampering him, sheltering him?"

"It's just that he's too much like his father. I loved his father, and I don't want to lose Harold Junior like I lost Harold Senior."

"I know, Paula. He's the exact image of his father. Why, he had that little girl last night strapped over like a . . ."

"What!" exclaimed Paula. "I know damn well that you didn't get Harold one of your prostitute girlfriends. You tell me you didn't, Harry."

"No, Paula, she was just a girl Harold met and wanted to spend some time with for his birthday, that's all."

"Well, Harold *has* a girl, and a baby, living in the housing projects while he's living a life of luxury. He is sure 'nough like you and his daddy. It's in the blood, in those genes of all you Simmons men, to break girls' hearts."

"I don't have time to discuss all that bullshit right now, Paula. The Three Stooges fucked up on their end, so go get Sylvia out of bed. I need her to cash a check for me."

"Okay, Harry, but when you get back over to that hotel, you tell Harold to come home. I made him a cake and bought him a new jogging suit."

"Okay, Paula. Now go get Sylvia."

"Sylvia's next door with her boyfriend. I'll call her on the phone."

Harry thought, she don't give a damn about Sylvia, but puts everything into whatever Harold is doing. Where is Harold? Who is Harold with? If she had spent more time with Sylvia, she wouldn't have become such a bitch nymphomaniac slut. That's why he didn't want to be bothered with women—they were from another planet! Just give him his tobacco farm and he'd be satisfied for the rest of his life. Mothers and their sons! He guessed his

117

own mother had been the same way, too, but she always liked Harold Senior better than him. Enough family history. He had to get down to business and make Sylvia some identification to cash these checks. The equipment was in the garage.

Harry searched the garage to find his identification photograph camera in the mounds of illegal gadgetry he had. He had been around a long time and knew every shortcut, from insurance fraud to staging a phony death with a certificate, complete with the purple seal from the coroner's office.

All this shit would have to go when he left this place. He'd get twenty years if he got caught with all those birth certificates and other AKA identifications. He was going to retire and didn't want any unwarranted luggage.

He began setting up the camera to make some identification for Sylvia so she could cash a few checks for him. That would give her something to do. After all, he'd have to pay her, too, when this thing was through, so she might as well earn her way like everyone else.

"Sylvia will be right with you, Harry. She's watching a movie with her new boyfriend next door."

"Tell her to put a rush on it. I got to get over to the post office before it closes to pick up all that computer equipment before one o'clock!"

"What do you want with Sylvia, anyway? She doesn't know anything about computers."

"Paula, you know damned well what I'm doing. It's part of Operation Parlay, and I don't have the time or patience to explain what I'm doing again," Harry said testily.

"Harry, why do you want to try to beat the system all the time? You've been doing it all your life."

"Paula, I need all the support I can get right now, so

don't give me your negativism."

"That corruption and that always wanting to get one over on somebody has cost you your twin brother's life. And you've been married more times than Elizabeth Taylor. Don't you know when it's time to stop all that foolishness and come down to earth?"

"Come down to earth? What the hell is on earth for you and me? Not a damned thing! The man owns everything, and he'll always control everything. What have you got to show after living for over fifty-five years? Not a damned thing. And everything I have, I didn't earn. I stole it! Yes, or I wouldn't have had anything in life and would probably be pushing a shopping cart like those guys living at the St. Vincent Mission."

"They've never done anything to you, Harry," said Paula. "You've been offered plenty of jobs, but you never accepted them because you couldn't take anyone telling you what to do. Just leave those corporate machines alone, Harry. You can't break them. It's part of the American system. You've parlayed your whole life, always trying to get enough money to break the backs of the corporate mega-buck world, just because they wouldn't accept you in their world. Leave it alone and stop speculating and investing your time and money." Paula walked away, upset, realizing for the past twenty-five years she'd been constantly arguing with Harry about what was right and what was wrong, but to no avail. Harry was a natural con artist and would always be one, no matter how much money he had or how many toys he had to play with. That garage was full of his toys, all things he'd used to corrupt and take things from the Big Machine. Time after time he only lived to get one over on The Man, whether the man was the IRS or the local city trash and sanitary department. He always challenged the system in court or by setting them up, basically blackmailing them. He was too old for that now, and now he was getting Harold Junior and Sylvia involved.

"Oh, Harry," Paula called out, "you have a message from John who works at the Union Plaza Hotel. I left his number on the kitchen counter. He said for you to call him as soon as you can." Paula slammed the door to her room and tried to control her anger.

Harold Junior was right, Harry thought. I never should have let my sister-in-law move in with us. Now I can see why my brother and her split up. She's a real bitch, and if she were mine, I'd . . .

"Uncle Harry?" A voice came from the front of the house. It was Sylvia and the baby. "Did you want me?"

"Yeah. Oh, let me hold little Charlene. Ain't she a living doll?" Harry said.

Sylvia knew right then and there that Harry wanted something from her. He never paid that little child any mind. Harry disliked children in general, and despised illegitimate children in his family and wanted to keep the family line strong with only good Southern blood and rich blue blood with green money.

"She's getting cuter and cuter, Sylvia."

"Uncle Harry, what do you want?" Sylvia said, placing her right hand on her hip as if she knew Harry's game plan.

"Oh, I just need a small favor, child. I want you to cash three checks for me and I'll make it very worth your while."

"How much, Uncle? My worth and my while are very precious to me these days. So how much?"

"Well, little darlin', how about your Uncle Harry giving you a thousand dollars just for cashing three checks for me?"

"Okay. Let's go right now. With that money Thomas and I can go to the Caesar's mall to shop, and I can buy him a special gift," Sylvia said, her eyes getting brighter and a smile on her face.

"Hold on, little filly. First I got to take a picture of you and laminate it on this Las Vegas driver's license."

"Uncle Harry, you're not up to your old tricks again, are you?"

"Why, what makes you think that?"

"Well, Mama told us only to trust you as far as we can see you, and when we can't see you, you're up to something," Sylvia said in a laughing manner.

"All right, I'll just call some other friends of mine to do this favor for me, and they can make a few extra dollars," Harry said, disappointed.

"No, no, I didn't say I wouldn't do it. I just said that my time is worth a lot these days, so let's get busy and cash those checks."

"Now that's what I want to hear. Let me take your picture, then we'll go to three separate check cashing places to cash these checks. Then I'll go down to the United Parcel Service and pick up my package."

"Sounds like a winner, Uncle."

"Okay, let's go."

Harry waited in the car as Sylvia cashed the first check without any problem. But on the second and third checks they ran into a snag. The manager knew that the I.D. was a forgery and had to get paid for cashing the checks under the table in cold cash. Harry went in and took care of the situation. The manager knew Harry and shook his head, as if he knew the City of Las Vegas was in trouble because the old King of the Crossroaders was back in action.

"Now let me have the rest of the money, Sylvia," he said as she got back into the car and placed the baby into her car seat in the back.

"That's all there is, Uncle Harry," Sylvia said.

"Now look. You are my niece, but I ain't no fool, and I'll break your arm just as fast as I would a prostitute who gets caught clipping me for my wallet. Now come up with the cash, and fast."

"Here. I don't think I was paid enough. I didn't know the checks were going to be for that much money. Why, you have over twenty-five thousand dollars there. Why can't I have more?"

"If you need more, why didn't you ask me, you little. . . . Well, I ain't going to call you that word, at least not in front of your face. You are my deceased brother's only girl kid, and you are my blood, so just ask me the next time you need money. Now here's an extra five hundred. Go buy your baby some Pampers and a few summer clothes."

"Thanks, Uncle Harry! Say, can you take me over to a friend of mine who lives in North Las Vegas? I owe him a few dollars, and . . ."

"No, sweet darlin'. I got to get to the UPS office right now. And you ain't got no friends in North Las Vegas. Were those same friends there when you and your mama got evicted? No. All you want to do is go buy some more of that drug. And if I pull up in North Las Vegas driving this 1938 Clinet, they ought to put me away, child. Get your new boyfriend to handle your compulsiveness by having some good sex. I can't help you."

Harry paid for the C.O.D. and drove home to wait for the UPS truck to arrive and the computer technician to set up the massive and extremely advanced computer system. The computer had the capability to launch a nuclear war missile just by using the correct codes of the Strategic Air Command. It could set off a missile in a nuclear submarine targeted at any country in the world. And the computer had the capability to transfer billions of dollars into accounts throughout banks all over the world. With that computer, Harry's confidence level ran high, and his compulsive behavior was at a boiling point. He could already imagine how sweet it would be on that tobacco farm, overlooking his plantation and workers. How sweet it would be.

He decided to call John at the Union Plaza to find out what he wanted while he was waiting. Harry hoped he wasn't in any trouble. The phone rang and someone answered.

"Yes, may I speak to John, please?" Harry said, making it sound like an official business call. "John, this is Mr. Simmons. My sister-in-law told me you called, and I thought I'd call and find out what's going on."

"Well, Mr. Simmons, I can't talk to you right now, but something big is getting ready to go down, and I'm being set up as a scapegoat, a patsy. I'll call you at your house on my break. Talk to you later." The line went dead. John's voice sounded frantic, and Harry hoped that this incident wouldn't interfere with Operation Parlay.

Suspecting me, I just can't believe it, I never stole nothing in my life—and just look at what they're doing, stealing from all these people that don't know no better, just taking their money and not returning a damn penny, John thought. Having been accused by the sport betting manager of stealing more than ten thousand dollars he was highly upset and disappointed; he had to speak to someone so he called Mr. Simmons, thinking that he would never get out of the casino alive. . . .

All of this money inside this here drawer; and I knew that something was going wrong, I could just feel it—those gangsters, they took the money out of the safe last night,

I bet. When I turned in my money bag—I handed that money bag to Mark, the night manager; why that dirty bastard. I bet that he never put that money inside the safe. I handed that money bag to him and he stuffed it away inside his jacket and now I'm the patsy, all the blame will be put on me!

John's emotions flared as he watched all the movement around the sports betting section of the casino and the pointing of the finger toward him.

They never even paid me; they owe me for two weeks wages; and I earned my money—what am I going to tell my wife? We may be evicted—look at me sweating and scared to death as if I did take the money, but I am completely innocent.

John, now listening and looking at the security guards questioning the manager and cashiers, leaned over his cash drawer and watched it pop open.

Look at all of this money, enough to pay my rent, buy the kids some school clothes and stop the old lady from yelling at me constantly—"You're not making no money at the casino," she'll say, "Go get another job at McDonald's"—Well, why don't she get off her fat ass and get her a job at McDonald's—but just look at all this money—well. I would rather deal with the Mafia than deal with her big mouth, besides, they already got me pegged as the thief and I ain't even had a trial; I'm the low man on the totem pole.

As John turned his back toward the camera, he leaned over his cash box, placed his right hand inside the one-hundred dollar slot, slipped and balled up all those one-hundred dollar bills, without hesitation.

They got me pegged as the thief and I need the money to feed my kids, besides, this money was gotten by illegal games—those runners, from the east coast, laundering drug money and stolen goods money, place their bets with this dirty, filthy money—betting one thousand dollars at a time, every race that come through that satellite big screen as they look at me like I ain't nothing—why, they made me look dirty; I'm the one that they are using, I touched that dirty drug money and placed it in this here money drawer—I better clean up all the fifty-dollar bills, that money is probably dirty, too.

John took all the fifty and one-hundred dollar bills and placed the dirty, and as he called it, dirty drug laundering, money inside his sock and then excused himself to use the toilet. He walked on the red and blue carpet with his head down to the ground, with the inkling that he dropped some of the money out of his socks. As he listened to the crunching of the money, he also heard the cheering of the race track betting, people cheering for their horse to come in at the Santa Anita race track on the big screen TV. Then, as he continued to hold his head down, as if he were ashamed of what he did, he could hear the coins dropping out of the slot machines, clack, clack, clack, clack, as if the player on that machine had won some big cash. The new people coming through the exiting door walked over to see what the player at the slot machine won, but in actuality, that player had only pushed the "Cash Out" button to redeem her winnings after putting ten times the amount of the pay-out inside the machine. John listened to the people at the crap table and walked toward the exit door as if he had taken a crap on himself, totally ashamed and bewildered by them accusing *him* of stealing when they planted people inside the casino to "get the crowd going," gave them casino money and told them to yell and shout out when someone sevens or elevens to draw more suckers in to play, to take a chance, knowing that there is no way out of a habit, an addiction, an obsession; John found a way out, he finally reached the back exit door and he ran for his life. . . .

*   *   *

The stage was set, and all seven parlay players were in place for the operation. This had to work, for the sake of his sanity, and so all the others would give him the necessary respect that he needed. One last time, one more sting, Harry thought to himself as he checked his list and made the calls to his constituents and confederates who would participate in the game—the game of getting over, the game of life, the game of survival.

If only things had been distributed equally in life, he could have made it in the mainstream of life, raised a family and retired like everybody else. But no, they tempted him and discriminated against him with all of their wealth and institutionalized tactics to bury him. But if he could just pull off this last operation, he'd see them all fall. If things worked out according to his plans, some corporate heads would roll. This would be even bigger than the Savings and Loan scandals.

Why was he putting his life and the lives of others at risk? Maybe Paula was right. He was hooked on winning, and he had reinvested his winnings all for this last big sting on those who had seen that the have-nots could get a little for themselves.

Maybe someday they will understand how corrupt Las Vegas was and how no one stood a chance to win. Maybe this sting would go down in history as being the greatest robbery since the French Connection, where no one was ever caught. Maybe he would be thought of as a modern-day Robin Hood. Well, they'd see. It was on for tomorrow. He had to get psyched out. The heat was on.

12

To parlay, as defined by Mr. Webster, was to bet an original amount and its subsequent winnings. Harry Simmons could not be outdone, and he redefined the term parlay to mean the use of one's money, talents or assets to obtain spectacular wealth or success.

And that he did, for Harry had invested six years in educating himself about computers and their limitations just to pull off one of the largest robberies of the century. Harry had invested every last penny he had in the planning, the design and the total operation of this plan. He had studied psychology to find out what made people tick; he wanted to know how people could be controlled to the point that they would take unnecessary risks just to protect an idea, a symbol, a moral or an ethic that they believed in. Harry knew people and their motives, and used his talents to mesmerize and hypnotize them into obeying his commands without any mistakes or errors.

Execution day was usually hot and humid in Las Vegas as all the players took up camp at Bally's Hotel and Casino.

"Why do you keep looking out the window, Harry? All the others will be here shortly," said Paula. She had never before seen Harry so nervous.

"It's not the players I'm worried about, Paula. Just between me and you, it's just that this may be the last time I gaze on the Las Vegas Strip. This may be the last time I ever feel the warmth of the desert sun, and this will probably be the last time I see you and my little family."

"Harry, you can't lose your confidence now. You must show the others that you're strong. After all, you're the one who got us involved in all this. We trust you, and to see you freeze up like this only makes people nervous. And when people get nervous, they get scared, and scared people can't win no money."

"You're right, Paula," Harry laughed. "Maybe if I do something constructive. . . . Yeah, I'll show everybody the layout on the slide projector. And, Paula, after this is over you'll find some deeds to the estate in the bedroom safe. You have the combination. My attorney has written out my will, and the property on Alta Street is to be divided among my kids and yours."

"Nothing's going to happen. Just get busy and explain the plan to everybody who's here now, while I freshen up our drinks."

"Okay," said Harry, adjusting the projector. "Here we are at Bally's Hotel." The five dancing girls, including Harold's girlfriend, Melinda, watched as the slide projector showed pictures from start to finish of the route that the caravan would take to the Mirage Hotel and Casino, ending at the valet parking.

"Now, here's the entrance. As each of you girls get out of the limo, start clanking and clinking those tambourines as loud as possible. In other words, create a scene," said Harry, sounding as if he were lecturing a classroom of freshman college students on the subject of cell biology. His slide show and points of concern were so detailed and graphic, they left no room for mistakes.

"The sheik's dancing girls will be in the first limo," he continued, "along with the Egyptian guitar players and the carpet layers. Remember, the Sheik of Armani is never allowed to step on 'unblessed' pavement or soil, so the two carpet rollers must always be in front of the sheik, or prince. Make sure the carpet is there before he steps out of the limo, and especially as he goes into the casino."

"Well, Harry, is the prince allowed to touch money or gambling chips? If he ain't, I'll handle them for him."

"Yeah, I bet you will." Everybody began to laugh.

"Benny, you and Sammy will be at the casino long before we arrive, setting up the stings at the blackjack tables and the dice table. Freddy, you must rig the slot machines. Not the twenty-five cent ones, the hundred-dollar machines. Are there any more questions?" Everybody responded no.

"Be sure to shield your costumes while you're loading up inside the limos so the employees here at Bally's won't suspect anything. Once they know that a billionaire sheik is in town, they'd bend over backwards for him to play at this casino.

"Now all I have to do is call ahead and notify them at the Mirage that the sheik, the prince, the heir to Armani, the richest oil-producing country in the world, has decided to arrive two days early due to a meeting with the oil cartel in Geneva. Everybody synchronize your watches."

"Harry, what time are we on? American time or Arabic time?" joked Sammy.

"Look, Sam, this is no time to joke around. You'll feel the pressure and the presence of insurmountable eyes and ears once you get inside the hotel. We're talking about making history here, Sammy. You'll be talked about for decades and will undoubtedly have more notoriety than the President or Michael Jackson, so let's get serious, okay?"

"Yeah, Harry. Loose lips sink ships."

*　　*　　*

Years later, Paula recalled how everything went down.

"Never had I seen such a perfectly planned operation, except maybe in that movie called *The Sting* with Paul Newman and Robert Redford. But this was live and in living color, and these people were real.

"Those five dancing girls were dressed up so fine, with their gold sequined outfits glittering and gleaming. And didn't Harold's girlfriend look cute with her princess crown and a red dot pasted on the middle of her forehead and wearing a veil? The interpreter Harry hired must have put him back a few bucks. He was so authentic and so real, I thought Harry must have imported him from Iran or Iraq, or one of those foreign countries where they got all of that money and oil.

"I felt like I belonged to something important, and I was a part of the program. My life finally had some meaning. From that point on, I knew why the Good Lord set me down on this planet. Oh, not to rob the Mirage Casino, but to be able to witness this fantastic and glamorous display of the most perfectly planned operation to ever take place on earth."

Paula recalled the whole thing, even back to when Harry started taking classes in computers and psychology at the University of Nevada, Las Vegas. Well, it was finally going to pay off for old Harry. But she had only one question—who was going to be the sheik, the prince? Surely not Harry. But as she watched him slip on his attire, she saw, yes, Harry was the sheik. She hoped he could get away with it. Although he resembled the Eastern man, he was far older-looking than that prince she'd seen in the newspaper. If Steve Flynn was in town and greeted Harry at the front of the Mirage, as he did with all of his VIP guests, they were in big trouble.

The belly rollers got into the first limo. She snapped at her son, Harold, because he almost blew the whole thing. He didn't want to let go of Melinda, and kept kissing her. Why, he acted as if he'd never had a girlfriend in his life, or at least not one like her. She must have really wiped it on that boy.

Freddy, Sammy and Benny drove ahead of the caravan to get those slot machines and dice and playing cards in place so the billionaire prince would be able to play with all of that oil money and clean out the Mirage with all of their illegal crossroader's trick gambling techniques.

And Paula? She fixed herself up so beautiful that it reminded her of when she was an aspiring actress in Hollywood. Her role was that of a news commentator, with a real microphone and a cameraman who had one of those big hollywood cameras; it looked real from the outside, but didn't have a thing inside it. Her job was to interview Harry, the billionaire prince, and also to handle some of the press release work. She was finally getting her chance to perform on a real stage. She was at the front of the parade when it arrived at the Mirage Hotel and Casino. The crowd of lookie-loos and passersby had already assembled as the three limos pulled up at the Mirage.

"Come on now, Hank," she told the cameraman, "stop lagging behind. The Prince of Armani has arrived, and you're still sitting on your extension cord. Now let's move it!" She was speaking as loud as she could so the other people who'd gathered would surely know that a big VIP was there at the Mirage and ready to play until he dropped a bundle of his oil money.

A motion picture? No way. Everything was rehearsed too perfectly. It was better than a movie as the five girls got out of the first limo, clapping and clanging those tambourines and playing that Arabic music while Joe, the cab driver, opened the doors for them. Those girls were just a-twistin' around, rolling their bellies and enticing the young men who were watching them. If Oscars were awarded for a good performance, those girls should have received them. They read their script well and put on a hell of a show as the camera switched to the second limo, where the interpreter and carpet rollers were getting out. Harold got to work, laying out that carpet for the prince as they had rehearsed it.

Bearing the flags of his country, the third limo pulled up and the crowd began to yell out as if Prince, the rock star, or Michael Jackson had arrived. The driver opened the door as the carpet was unrolled, and out stepped the prince. Trumpets sounded and the bodyguards and interpreter stood on the side. All you could see were the shoes, white, then the pure silk socks, and then the leg and pants of pure gold. It was spectacular the way the sun reflected off the pure gold pants. Everyone had to shield their eyes. People began to crowd and push just to get a glimpse of the prince.

Wearing an outfit fit for a king, Harry, the prince, emerged from the limo, bowing and then kissing the carpet that had been unrolled, asking his interpreter in some kind of language that they had concocted which was east and which way was west, for it was time to pray.

The interpreter responded in a language that only Harry (the prince) could understand, and then they proceeded through the gold doors of the Mirage Hotel and Casino.

"Why Prince Karimani of Armani, we thought that

you would be arriving on Friday, not Wednesday," the hotel manager and administrator said. The prince's interpreter intercepted any communications between the prince and others who wished to talk to His Royal Highness.

"The prince says that you were informed of the change of schedule and that the prince has some urgent business in Geneva with the oil cartel and must fly back to Armani. Is not the hotel and casino open twenty-four hours a day, seven days a week?" the interpreter said, as the prince (Harry) commented in his special language.

"Yes, of course, we're always open for your Royalness, but there is a question of security, sir. Steve Flynn, the owner, is out of town on business," the casino manager said.

Through the interpreter, Harry replied, "I had previously met Mr. Flynn, a most charming fellow. But as I just discussed with you, I have urgent business to attend to, so escort me to the casino at once. It is hotter than the Sahara Desert out here."

The casino administrator thought, Isn't he used to temperatures over 120 degrees? but paid it no attention and escorted the prince inside the Mirage.

"Here is the prince's itinerary. Please pay close attention to the gaming or gambling, and—a word that the prince does not like to use—the schedule. The prince will have the same accommodations as before and, by the way, here are the banking codes that the prince has to authorize him to withdraw funds to play. Now, can you direct us to the cashiers, please?"

"But don't you want to freshen up a bit? I don't mean to insult your Highness, but that was a long plane ride, and we have all the accommodations for the prince at his disposal. . . ."

The prince replied angrily, stomping his foot, and the interpreter told the casino administrator, "You have just insulted the prince and his country. Mr. Flynn will be hearing from his Embassy. How dare you tell the prince of the richest and most productive country of oil in the world that he stinks? Don't you know that the prince has a royal bathtub inside his cabin on his 787 jet? Now, get the prince a million dollars in one-hundred-dollar coins immediately to play the slot machines, the hundred-dollar slots. Also immediately get the prince a rolling cart to push the million dollars, or he will go over to Caesar's Hotel and Casino."

The casino manager hastily sputtered, "Oh, I apologize profusely to the Prince. If you would just sign here . . ." He gave paper and pen to the interpreter. " . . . we will roll the million dollars out immediately."

Paula thought to herself, after living all her life in the United States, it was the first time she felt equal to the dominant culture, just because of what the King of the Crossroaders, her brother-in-law, was doing to set the record straight. That feeling of finally having enough money to buy a half-gallon of milk, and of rubbing elbows with the same people she considered as well-dressed with rich mannerisms excited the hell out of her. To this point, she'd thought racism stemmed from the whites not letting blacks have equal jobs and equal pay. But it wasn't that at all. Prejudice and racism stemmed from those who had money towards those who didn't. And when somebody didn't have that green stuff, that's what divided cultures and placed barriers on obtaining the essentials in life.

Just a few years ago, the people who lived in those foreign oil countries were living in worse poverty than the blacks who lived in the most deprived areas and ghettos in the South of the old Delta. Then they discovered black gold, and now look at them. They were an accepted culture throughout the world. That oil upgraded their culture and gave them billions of dollars. It wasn't their religion or their color, it was that oil.

How come nobody discovered black gold on some poor black person's property? She guessed they were meant to be slaves all their lives here on earth, and nothing would change that.

Harry had to psych himself out when he signed for that million dollars in hundred-dollars chips, as he and his entourage walked over to the hundred-dollar slot machine. His stomach started yearning and turning.

"We'll clear the area so you can play, your Highness," the casino administrator said.

"No, no," said Harry's interpreter. "The Prince of Armani wants to mingle with the American people. That's the reason he decided to take this short vacation. He's tired of being trapped in the bureaucracy. Let the people watch and enjoy themselves," he said. Harry knew damn well that he had to have a crowd around in order for Sammy, Benny and Freddy to do their thing and tilt the odds in his favor.

Paula's job was now as reporter and transcriber, taking notes and jotting down the whole event, since the Gaming Commission did not allow cameras or tape recording devices inside the casino. Her job was to maintain the public's interest and draw more of a crowd there to obscure what Freddy was going to do with the slot machine, and that was to "tilt" that chip inside the Mega-Buck payoff machine to pay the Prince of Armani.

Everything was preprogrammed. Freddy handled a device strapped on his hip to give signals to Sylvia and Thomas, stationed at the headquarters at the house. Sylvia and Thomas received the code number of the exact slot machine that the Prince of Armani was playing, and then they would program in that number from that chip inside the slot machine and jumble and cross the tumbler numbers by blocking the main Mega-Buck payoff computer in Reno, Nevada. Harry had everything planned, and figured with that complex Soviet computer he could reprogram the specific dates and times of the big payoffs in his favor.

Freddy punched in the code and it was relayed to Sylvia and Thomas at the house. Thomas then punched those numbers into the telephone modem, and that was transferred to Reno, where the Gaming Commission and all of the Mega-Buck payoffs from each and every multi-million dollar payoff was hooked up. That signal was then relayed back to Las Vegas into the electronic computer chip of the machine Harry was playing, causing it to hit the tumblers of that computer chip, and then. . . .

All they heard were bells ringing! Honey, it was like New Year's Day when that three-and-a-half million dollar slot machine payoff hit! It was one of the largest payoffs of its kind in the history of casino gambling.

The casino administrator and a few of his agents ran over to the slot machine to calculate the winnings, and sure enough, the highlights from that digital display were correct. The Prince of Armani had just won over three million dollars.

"Close this machine down immediately!" the casino administrator ordered, looking disgusted and humiliated.

Just then, Paula knew that what Harry had been telling her all this time was true. All of that "baiting in" of gamblers and all the lights and sounds coming out of those machines was nothing but a fantasy, an illusion projected for suckers. She could tell from the expression on the manager's face that there was no way for that machine to pay off at that particular time. It was only Uncle Harry's interference that made that machine light up like a Christmas tree, that made that slot machine pay off.

Las Vegas, the land of pipe dreams and fantasy. Boy, did they take a lot of people for their lives' earnings. Those old ladies, Social Security recipients and county welfare recipients like she used to be, were the casino's favorite friends.

The Prince of Armani then switched to the twenty-five dollar slot machines as the crowd gathered around. Freddy got behind that machine with his miniature computer and sent another signal to Sylvia and Thomas, who programmed those signals to the main Mega-Buck progressive payoff in Reno. The Reno computers went into a dead stop, and the computer technician in Reno jumped out of his chair and got on the phone to notify the Chamber of Commerce and the Gaming Commission that there had been another payoff within five minutes coming out of Las Vegas, something very unusual, the technician said.

"Usually we get one from Laughlin and one from Reno or one of those small-town gambling casinos in Nevada, but Chief, this is coming straight out of Las Vegas, just like the last big one just five minutes ago."

"Run a tracer on it and find out the exact gambling casino so we can fly in an investigation team."

"Okay, Chief. But to run that tracer will take me at least thirty minutes. Why, this computer hit a dead stop, and I got to get this software rolling again. Chief, I've never seen anything like it. It's as if someone put the brakes on the program wheels and it's running itself."

"Just put the tracer on it and let me know what the payoffs were."

"Got you, Chief. Oh, Chief, both payoffs were Mega-Buck, progressive, and I can give you an estimate of ten million. . . . "

The Prince of Armani knew that there was no time to waste, so he gave the signal to Freddy to let a few other machines pay off to create another illusion so the casino managers and administrators would scramble. Freddy knew what the signal meant and walked around to the low-budget machines to set them off.

"Never before have so many people been served with so little," Paula said to herself. Now she saw how it was done. Those slot machines were pre-programmed and knew exactly when to pay off by computers. How could she have been so naive?

The interpreter and the casino administrator talked about how the prince wanted his money.

"You are to transfer all of the winnings into this account in Switzerland immediately," said the interpreter.

"Certainly. And will the prince be playing the slot machines any more today?" asked the administrator hopefully.

"No, the prince has decided to play with the dice. And he wants a receipt and a confirmation number that the funds have been transferred, please."

"Of course. I'll have the accountants prepare to transfer the 8.7 million dollars immediately, sir. And the prince will be playing with the remaining two-and-a-half million?"

"That is correct. He will be playing with the remaining two-and-a-half million, and then he will dine," said the interpreter.

Harry then gave the order to block the transfer of the funding into the Swiss account and transfer that funding into his account in Venezuela, where his tobacco farm

139

would be located. Freddy got the message and typed that message in to Sylvia and Thomas at the main computer headquarters.

"Break the computer down after the transfer. We won't be needing it any longer." Freddy tilted his head and it was no sooner said than done. When that money got transferred, that main computer caused such a friction on that hot day in July that Las Vegas had a brown-out. All the power all over the city was blinking, and the power went completely off on all the slot machines for a few minutes. That Soviet computer sure enough had a lot of power, and Harry knew exactly how to program that big sucker.

They had already made over twelve million dollars, and the Prince of Armani was still winning at the craps table, where the limits were none.

13

"Harry's a bigger fool than I thought he was," muttered Benny to himself as he watched from the other end of the dice table. He'd already made off with at least twelve million dollars. What more did he want? As soon as these dice got slow, he was asking for his share and getting the hell out of there.

The Prince of Armani (AKA Harry Simmons) placed ten thousand dollars in the field of the crap table as Benny looked on and got the signal from Harry to make a switch on the first roll.

"Coming out...coming out...no point," the stick man yelled out as the Prince of Armani tossed the two dice so hard and far that everyone looked on the floor and wondered where the dice had gone. Benny caught the one die and made the switch to an "all cube six die" while the other die was found by the place bet dealer on the craps table. The stick man looked at the dice just briefly and used the stick to shove them within the prince's reach. The first roll was a twelve, a number that was a nasty crap for the ones who had confidence in the prince. On the other hand, the prince tripled his winnings in the field and told his interpreter to "let the money ride."

The next roll was a nine, and the field won again; the prince had over fifty thousand dollars in the field and rolled another twelve, which paid triple. He let the money ride and then rolled another double six. The chips were stacked up so high that they had to cart in another wagon of black hundred-dollar playing chips. That's when the prince gave Benny the signal that he was going to throw the house a curve, and there it went. That one die disappeared, and Benny made the switch again to the original die that he had stored in his short sleeve.

"Close down the table and gather the prince's winnings," the administrator of the casino said as he escorted the prince to the cashier's table. The prince then informed them that he wanted his winnings of more than eight hundred and eighty-five thousand dollars in cash, and the prince and his entourage walked over to the blackjack table.

It was hard to believe that so much money could be won in so little time, Paula thought as she observed Harry and feared for her life. When was he going to stop? She hoped after the blackjack game he'd call it quits. Enough is enough, and judging from those surveillance cameras up there, Harry's picture was being taken and they'd already run a make on him. They'd all be put in jail. What more did he want? Was Harry truly trying to break Las Vegas? He should quit while he was ahead. You couldn't break these casinos, especially when you were playing with their money.

As the prince walked up to the blackjack table, he said not a word, just observed the players until he spotted Sammy. The casino administrator ordered the whole blackjack section to be closed down and then he gave the signal to bring in the best blackjack dealer in the house, one with a fast hand so the casino could retrieve their money.

"The Prince of Armani wants to be with the American people. Let them be," said the interpreter. The casino administrator told the security guards not to bother with closing the blackjack section down.

The prince looked like he was tired after staying up all night, planning and thinking about how he would get the cash out of the casino. Then it dawned on him. He would tell his interpreter to tell the casino administrator to carry the game of blackjack to the Executive Suite, alone with all of his winnings—in cash, some six million dollars—and eleven million dollars already transferred by computer wire. The administrator agreed.

The plan was for the prince to freshen up in his private suite after playing a few hands of blackjack and then go to the Executive Suite and play poker on the twelfth floor of the casino hotel.

Sammy was the fall guy at the end of the blackjack table and knew from playing blackjack for over fifty years the exact probability of each card being dealt. If he didn't get the right card, he would create an illusion, like spilling his drink on the table or reflecting his diamond ring into the eyes of the blackjack dealer. The prince sat down and placed a ten-thousand-dollar bet and the casino manager okayed it, after being given the okay from the casino administrator.

The heat was on as everyone looked on. The Prince of Armani was completely exhausted. The hand was dealt and the prince received a king's ransom; a king showing and a king down. The prince decided to go double and the casino administrator authorized the bet. Ironically, the prince received another king and a deuce. The Prince wanted to triple his bet and hit the remaining kings. On all three kings the prince received a total on each play of twenty. Now, if only the dealer would either bust out or receive less than twenty, the prince would make over thirty thousand dollars on one single hand.

Sammy made certain of that because, as he esti-mated, if the dealer had to hit and received a nine with two showing, the dealer would have a twenty-one and would beat the Prince of Armani with one card and receive a per-fect twenty-one. Sammy took a hit to mix up the deck, and it worked, since the dealer took a hit, which was a four. Sammy received the nine that would have given the dealer a perfect twenty-one. If the next card the dealer received was anything higher than a five, he would bust out and the prince would win.

But the dealer had to take another hit. The next card was a seven, and the dealer lost. The crowd rejoiced and there was laughter all over the casino. People really enjoyed seeing someone win against the odds, even if it was a billionaire.

The prince left the winnings on the table, and Sammy threw in the card just right for the prince to receive a blackjack, which pays double and a half.

The exhaustion was unbearable, and Harry knew he couldn't take it any longer, so he signaled his interpreter to tell the casino administrator that it was time that he retired to his room. The whole crew of five dancing girls, three bodyguards, one interpreter, three con artists (Sammy, Benny, and Freddy), Paula, Harold, and Joe, the driver, retreated to the room, all at separate times, along with seven carts full of money.

*   *   *

"Harry, what's wrong? Are you all right?" Paula asked, looking at Harry like he was having a heart attack.

"I'll be all right, Paula. Get me the money so I can pay the crew so they can take the next plane out of the city."

144

The money carts were lined up along with the blackjack winnings. An estimated seventeen million dollars was won at the Mirage Hotel and Casino in just seven hours.

"They're onto us by now, so the rest of us will have to escape from here using plan B. We won't have time to gamble at Caesar's, so let's get busy and get out of here quick."

Benny, Harry's long-time confidante, received a handsome one million seven hundred and fifty thousand dollars and a brand new Samsonite suitcase to put the money in. Sammy and Freddy received their shares of the lot, an estimated million dollars each, and all three pulled their new Samsonite suitcases out of the room and wept tears of joy, since they knew that they'd probably never again see the King of the Crossroaders.

Harry was sad, but had to keep on distributing the money before Security came up the hall to arrest them. Mohammed, the interpreter, received his hundred and seventy-five thousand dollars, and complained to Harry that he should have received more for his act.

"You're going to receive a twenty-year jail term if you don't get the hell out of here right now. They're onto you, so get lost!" Harry said. He couldn't take any chances. There was no honor among thieves. He put into action the alternative escape plan.

"Now, all of you listen and listen carefully. The rest of you are family, or like my family. Everybody grab a duffel bag and fill it with money. We'll go to the top of the Mirage, where a large crane will be hoisted up to us; it's used to place the trash inside while they're building the new Treasure Island Hotel. We'll all jump inside the trash chute. There's a Star bus waiting for us to the right. Just get inside the bus and change into something casual. Put the money in the back of the bus inside the seats that open up. Now, you got the instructions?"

"Yeah, Harry, so let's move!"

Never had a robbery been so well-planned, and so well executed. They left the room three at a time—Harold, Melinda and Paula up the fire escape and down the trash chute, then three of the dancing girls up the fire escape and down the trash chute. The three bodyguards, all carrying with them duffel bags of money, followed close behind. Joe and Harry remained.

Harry left an envelope addressed to Steve Flynn, with a typed letter inside, saying, JUST LOVE STAYING AT YOUR HOTEL AND THE COMP MONEY. SEE YOU REAL SOON, STEVE. LOVE AND KISSES . . . A NEW CORPORATE OWNER OF THE MIRAGE HOTEL AND CASINO.

Joe and Harry then went up the fire escape and down the trash chute and got on the bus. Everybody was quiet as they sat in their seats.

"Okay, we're all here. So why is everybody so quiet? Is the money in the back of the bus in the seats as I instructed?"

"Yes, Harry."

"So, what's wrong?"

"It's just that everybody's in a state of shock. They've never seen anything so perfectly executed and planned out without you even opening your mouth in there. It was fantastic!" said Paula.

"Let's go, Joe," ordered Harry. Joe started the engine on the $200,000 Star bus that was once Wayne Newton's tour bus. Harry had purchased it just for this occasion. "Oh, and Joe, you'll find the slip and the registration of your new bus in the window visor. Have a good time with it! Now, let's all have a party!"

Everybody was happy that the plan was successful,

but it wasn't over yet. They still had to get out of town. Harry would take a jet to Los Angeles, then to Venezuela, where he'd purchased a tobacco farm. Paula was finally going back to Atlanta, where she was born, and Joe, the cab driver, was going to Aspen, Colorado, to be with his daughter and grandchildren. The rest of the crew hadn't decided yet and just hung around the estate for a few days and watched the news that reported "the heist of the century."

The hotel owners stated that more than 30 million dollars was stolen by a billionaire sheik impersonator who was planning to launder some illegal weapons money with a loan from the United States Government. Just a few faces could be seen on the casino cameras, and the Federal Bureau of Investigation was looking into the case.

Harold and Melinda decided to go live in sunny Florida with their combined hundred and seventy-five thousand dollars. Before they left, Uncle Harry made Harold give his former girlfriend twenty-five thousand so she and the baby could find a new place to live.

When Paula got her money, she didn't know what to do. Harold had gone, and Sylvia was always with that new boyfriend of hers. Paula stayed in Las Vegas a little longer, bored to death, and with money to burn. She became obsessed with watching soap operas, and that was even more depressing.

Harry took off for his undisclosed location tobacco farm, where he wrote and told them he was "living large."

14

I have to find something to do with my life, Paula thought. She had to sit around in Vegas until the house sold, and the economy was really slow. Harry had given specific instructions about what to do with the house and the money, so she had to see to it, after all that Harry had done for them. Sylvia had over seventy-five thousand dollars from Harry before he left, and she was planning on getting married to this new boyfriend of hers and buy a home.

Sometimes Paula heard from Benny up in Northern California, managing his wine orchards that he'd purchased with the money he received in Operation Parlay. But she seldom, if ever, heard from Sammy and Freddy. She guessed they were doing okay, and it was usually when you heard from people that you knew something was wrong. She figured Benny had overinvested in that grape business, and his crops had gone bad because of the spell of bad weather they'd had recently. He was trying to find out where Harry was, but she told him that when Harry called, she'd just give him the message.

While watching the news, she could have sworn she saw Freddy during that big rainstorm, his house dangling off a cliff, ready to fall into the ocean in Santa Cruz. The fellow complained he didn't have any disaster insurance, and his house was his retirement home he'd purchased with his life savings.

Well, it looked like what goes around comes around in

life, and the only one who was having good luck with their newly acquired fortune was Harry. Harry sent pictures of his tobacco farm and was trying to get her to come visit him, but she couldn't leave, at least not yet. She had to sell the house and take care of her granddaughter.

That Sylvia was back on drugs again, she just knew it. She was losing weight, and every time she saw her she was going to her room to get her bankbook. She prayed she wouldn't get that nice young man next door involved in those drugs. Once you used that cocaine one time, it was hard to get off that stuff. Smoking that cocaine became an obsession, and people who used it became compulsive and couldn't quit. She done told Sylvia over and over again. . . .

There she went again, into her room. Paula was willing to bet she was going to get more money.

"Sylvia, is that you, honey?" asked Paula.

"Yes, Mother. I forgot something in our room."

"Sylvia, I don't care what your Uncle Harry told you about this house being your home. I'm not going to have you run in and out all times of the night getting money."

"It's my money, and I'll spend it like I damn well please."

"Now I know you're on those drugs, talking to me that way. What happened to the agreement we made? We swore we would never go back to that compulsive gambling and drug use again. Just look at you. You've lost weight, and your hair looks like you been sleepin' in a barn. Tomorrow I'm going to take you to see a drug counselor, so don't go lay up all night with that boy. You better come home tonight and stop wasting your money on those cheap hotel rooms."

Sylvia glared at her mother and slammed out of the house.

There she goes again, Paula thought, in and out all times of night, smoking that cocaine. I can't even talk to her when she's on those drugs. She looks just like a zombie with those big eyes and clothes that smell like shit. She's gone all the way downhill since she got all of that money.

Suddenly, she had an idea. She'd take all of her money out of their room and put it away, so Sylvia couldn't find it. Paula went to Sylvia's room and hunted around. She thought back to the time when Sylvia used to hide a glass pipe under her mattress that she used to smoke cocaine with.

She found the money in an envelope in her dresser. "Why, there's only eleven thousand dollars in here!" she exclaimed. She sure as hell hoped she had more money in the room someplace else. She knew damn well that Harry had given her over fifty thousand dollars. Where was the rest of the money? That stupid-ass bitch wasn't that stupid, giving all her money to the dope man. Or was she? Well, she wasn't going to get this money, that was for sure.

Paula took the money and was walking toward the kitchen when she heard the telephone ring. It was Harold calling from Florida.

"Harold! Hi, honey, how are you and Melinda?"

"Mother," Harold said, "I'm in jail and need some money to get out."

"What? Why, what happened?"

"It's a long story, and I'll explain it to you when and after you bail me out of this lousy jail. I'm coming back home."

"Harold, where's Melinda?" Paula asked in a frightened manner.

"I had to send her back to India. She was playing around on me, Mother. I just couldn't satisfy her needs.

She had a compulsive sexual behavior that I just couldn't handle, and that's one of the reasons I'm here in jail."

"Okay, baby, I'll wire you the money. What jail are you in and how much do you need?"

"Mama, I need a hundred thousand dollars, but they'll drop the bail down to ten thousand and you can use the house for collateral."

"What? Son, you know I can't use the house. It belongs to all you kids and Harry's kid."

"Well, I guess I'll just have to rot in this jail cell along with these Cubans and Haitians. They all want to have sex with me, Mom."

"What! Okay, I'll send the money and anything else you need. But what happened to the $175,000 that Uncle Harry gave you, and the new Mustang?"

"Oh, Mother, I had some other problems that I'll explain to you when I get home."

"Problems ain't the word for it. You musta had a catastrophe, son. The next-door neighbor will drive me over to the bail bondsman here in Las Vegas, and they'll make the bail, so you just be patient."

"Okay, Mom. And Mother, I love you."

"I love you, too, Harold. I'll have you out of there by tomorrow."

What an idiot, Paula thought. She was willing to bet that little fool got involved in dealing drugs, and some of those Cubans and Haitians took his money and his girlfriend. He didn't have the brains he was born with. Damn, he'd blown his $175,000 in a matter of only a month and a half, that idiot, that compulsive drug dealer and hustler. This was it. She couldn't keep on giving her money to those kids. She'd have nothing left and would hit rock bottom, right back to the housing projects.

Sure, she did a little slot machine playing at the market every now and then, but she didn't spend all of her money. She wasn't a compulsive slots player.

Shit, let that idiot spend the night in jail. That would teach him a lesson. Anybody who spent over $175,000 in a month and a half deserved to be locked up in jail, or in a mental asylum! This was ridiculous!

She called a cab to drive her to the market. She had to get out her frustration at the slot machines. Why, the other day she'd won over a hundred dollars. But she didn't want to think about what she'd lost.

She still had plenty of money left, but tomorrow Harold, Sylvia, and she would be going to Gamblers' Anonymous, and when they finished with that, they were going to Narcotics Anonymous. Yeah, that's what they would do before it was too late.

*   *   *

Harold muttered to himself, "I knew things wouldn't go right." He paced the floor of the jail cell. "That damn bitch set me up and took the money and ran. After all I did for her, I just couldn't satisfy her." She was a pure nymphomaniac, with a compulsive desire for sex and spending money. He should have known better than to take a sleuth like her to Florida, where all those multi-millionaires came just to vacation. Now all he had was thirty-five thousand left in the Bank of Nevada. But what good would that do him in the Florida State jail?

With the charges that they had on him, he might never get out of there. They'd found ten kilos of pure cocaine in his Mustang. They planted it there; that was the only alibi he could come up with. This was his first Federal arrest; maybe they'd give him a break. Sure. Anytime they saw a young black boy driving a brand-new high-performance automobile, they were out to get him.

People were afraid of young black men because of what they saw on television, all of that dope dealing and killing that those cameras zoomed in on. In real life, it was another story. We aren't all like that, he thought angrily. Just because we were born into this world a certain color doesn't mean we're automatically guilty.

This jail was full of Puerto Ricans and Haitians, and he could see there was no hope for them. They couldn't even speak good English, and all they did was steal and rob people. But it was the environment they came from that made them like that. He knew that, personally. He knew what it was like to live in poverty, having to deal with junkies, living with cockroaches. These punk-ass Puerto Ricans and Haitians probably thought he was a square, a pansy-ass boy, but just let them try him. He'd whip their asses real good. The thieves, the drunks, the homosexuals, they'd better not bother him. He'd kill them, and they knew it.

"Hey, Amigo."

"What?" said Harold. "Are you talking to me?"

"Yeah, man. I was watching and listening to the sheriff when they brought you in here. Ten kilos is a lot of time, man. You're looking at twenty years, amigo."

"That was a set-up. I had no drugs in my vehicle. They put those drugs in my car," Harold said earnestly.

"That's what they all say, amigo. You see, my friend, any time they see a young black or brown boy with a new car driving to this part of Florida, it only spells one thing, and that is D–R–U–G–S. That's the only reason why people like yourself, of your age, come to this town, and that is to cop drugs, amigo."

153

"Well, they got it all wrong. I was just looking for a place to cool out, me and my lady, and they stopped us and confiscated my car."

"Can't your lady post bail, my friend?"

"No, she got scared and left. She hasn't even contacted me, and I've been sitting in this jail for two days."

"Where you from, amigo?" said the Puerto Rican.

"Las Vegas. And my name is Harold, not amigo."

"Las Vegas. That's the Gold Country, the land of opportunity and risk-takers. Yeah, amigo, or Harold."

"Yeah, it has its moments, and I wish I was there right now instead of this jail."

"Hey, amigo, how about that heist someone pulled off in Vegas a few months ago? They made off with over thirty million dollars. That was a lot of dinero!"

"Yeah, I heard about that." Harold thought before answering. "Las Vegas is a place that's always getting robbed. There's so much money there that people get tempted. Even the casino employees steal and risk their jobs and lives."

"One day I'll go to Las Vegas and try my luck," said Jose, for that was the Puerto Rican's name.

"If I can ever get out of this nasty hellhole, I'll go back to Las Vegas and never return to Florida," Harold muttered, staring at the ground as if he had lost something.

"What are you looking for, amigo, er, Harold? You dropped something, maybe?" asked Jose.

"Yeah, I dropped all my money, my car, and my girl-friend, all in one day. This is worse than living in North Las Vegas."

"Money? You lose some money here in Florida, my friend?"

"Yes, I had fifty thousand dollars inside my car when

they took me to jail, and I hope that my girlfriend has found it. Probably not. She probably found it and ran off with it."

"Hey, amigo, what's a young kid like you doing with all that dinero? Don't you know that you are lucky, my friend, that you are in jail instead of in the cemetery."

Harold thought about what Jose said and felt that he was talking sense, and he could probably discuss his problems with Jose in confidence. No, Harold thought again. I better not tell this stinking Puerto Rican anything about my family. He might be an informer. Besides, he was the only one in there who spoke English, and he was prying pretty hard to get information out of him.

Just like his mother had told him when he was younger, "Only trust someone as far as you can see them." And Uncle Harry, too. I learned a lot from him. He taught me how to study people's personalities, and always taught me to be wary of smiling faces.

Why, Harold thought, he was heir to the throne now that Uncle Harry was gone. He would be the King of the Crossroaders someday, as soon as he made a game plan and could get back to Las Vegas. He learned the hard way and got a piece of the good life. He wanted more of it—champagne, women, fast cars. He had to get back and take over his turf, his domain, his family fortune.

He must have been a fool to drive all the way here to Florida with all that money and that India bitch. He was blind in love, but now he knew the value of money. Once you lost it, you knew its value, and he'd lost a great deal of it.

Harold sat down and checked out his fellow inmates' personalities.

"Hey, amigo," a voice whispered, as if a candle were

being blown out, soft and very slowly. "You know, my friend," Jose said, "we can work out some sort of an agreement."

"Agreement on what?" Harold responded hesitantly, as if he had to show the Puerto Ricans and the Haitians housed in that jail cell that he was no sissy. "Where are you coming from? What the hell do we have to agree upon?"

"Getting out of here, my friend, or should I say, Harold," Jose said with an arch smile.

Harold's ears tuned in as if they were satellite dishes, trying to adjust to pick up the message while avoiding all the other inmates from listening. "You got a way out of this hellhole of a jail, Jose?"

"Si, amigo, but for a handsome price, my friend."

"The price, what is the price, Jose?"

"Aw, you remembered my name. You are more clever than I once thought you were, Harold."

"Tell me now, how do I get out of this place, and what is the price I have to pay for freedom?"

"That depends, friend Harold," Jose said with a hideous grin on his face showing three missing teeth and the rest rotted to the core.

"Look, be straight up front with me, and I'll be straight up front with you. What is the price of a ticket to get the hell out of here?"

"Like I said, my friend Harold, it depends on you and how far you must go. You see, amigo, you can escape right outside these gates, but you will be a dead man, my friend, by the time it takes for a hot lady of the evening to get you off."

"Come on, Jose, be up front with me." By then Harold was using what little gift he had of the Simmons bloodline and his gift of gab to talk up a good agreement.

"Well, Harold, what I'm saying is if the snakes don't get you, the posse will, in a manner of no time."

"Snakes, posse. Look, Jose, I need safe passage at least to the airport, where I can get you whatever money you need. Just get me there."

"Ah, money. Now you're singing my song, amigo. You say that you have money, my friend, and it is at the airport. Ten thousand pesos, my friend, to get you out, and ten thousand to get you to the airport."

"Safe and sound, my fine friend. You will get your money if I get to the airport safe and sound," said Harold as he made an agreement and shook his new-found friend's hand to guarantee the safe package to freedom. "And look, my fine friend, you know if any of your compadres fuck with me, the deal is off, and that ten thousand will be just a memory."

"Si, amigo. Now let me tell you what the plan is. When the Haitians get their recreation time in the yard, you and I will go out to the yard with them. Near the water hole there is soft ground, my friend, from the wastewater. We have dug under and made it possible for a skinny amigo like you to slide under the gate. You just follow me, my friend, and run as if you are running a race, a race for your life, amigo!"

"When is it time to go, my fine friend, Jose?"

"Tomorrow, at noontime, we will slip under the gate, and then hide in the brush of the everglades until the sun goes down. Now, the money, amigo, at the airport. There is where your part comes in. You must have a key. Let me see the key, amigo."

"Don't worry, my friend, you will see the key and the money in due time. Just get me there safe and sound and then we will be true friends. You got me?"

"Si, my friend. We will be brothers if we survive those

alligators in the swamps that we must cut through."

"Wait a minute. Swamps, alligators, snakes? Just where and how far do we have to travel?" Harold asked in desperation.

"Not far and not long, Harold. Think of it as an adventure, my young friend, and we will be there in no time."

"Yeah, we'll make it an adventure, an adventure in the everglades."

The art, the skill and the suggestive ability to smoothly coerce and connive an individual came to light from the dark as Harold talked up a good game and convinced Jose, his newly-acquired friend, that the cash-for-freedom game was real and the safe-and-sound commitment of getting Harold out of the jail facility in one piece was even greater.

"Damn!" Harold said to himself. He just remembered that if his mother called or sent the bail money, that would expose him. When they'd booked him, he'd used his father's name and his old I.D. If Paula called or posted bail, they'd know his real name and identification. He needed to call her back right away, but there was a line to use the phone, and it would take hours to get the call through. Maybe if he talked to Jose, he could convince him to let his people get in and make a quick phone call.

"Say, Jose, let me rap to you, my friend. That phone over there, I must use it."

"What?" Jose was catching a few Z's. "Si, amigo, I will tell my compadres that you must use the phone for emergency purposes." Jose talked to them, and the phone was at Harold's disposal.

Unfortunately, Paula wasn't home, so Harold had to leave a message. "Mother, this is Harold. Disregard everything I told you earlier today. I've made my own personal arrangements. See you in a few days. Love, Harold." He hoped she got the message, or at least didn't post bail. . . .

15

During that same afternoon, Harry was in his own little world on his tobacco farm, overseeing the workers. He sat on the front porch of his Carusa estate, nestled among the pastures of some of the richest tobacco on this side of the Colombian tobacco groves.

"What a fine afternoon," Harry said as he inhaled deeply. He exhaled suddenly, as the air was suddenly foul. Harry's lungs became irritated due to the spraying of pesticides on the tobacco. "Damn, if those cigarettes don't kill you, those pesticide chemicals will. What the hell do they spray on that tobacco, anyway?" It wasn't his problem. He was just there to relax and make a profit off his investment, not to ask questions about the chemicals sprayed on the tobacco.

His two-hundred acre plantation had cost him a bundle; it was a reinvestment of all his life's work and the grand finale of Operation Parlay. Paula and the rest of them hadn't believed that he could pull it off, but it was all a matter of timing, precise and exact timing, and now those corporate M.B.A. bigwigs were still looking for the robbers, along with the FBI, by now. But he'd covered his tracks too well. They would never find him.

It looked like a visitor was driving up the road. He didn't expect anyone that day and wondered who it could be. As he watched the vehicle approach the front of the house, Harry sipped his lemonade and watched the workers plow the tobacco fields.

It was that damn nosy sheriff. What the hell could he want this time?

"How do, Sheriff? It's certainly a fine day today. Will you join me in some cold lemonade?"

"Sí, Señor Manuel. I don't mind if I do." Sheriff Sanchez stepped out of the Jeep, pulling out his handkerchief and wiping the sweat and dust from his brow that had accumulated while driving to the estate. "Those chemicals, Señor Manuel, they no good for the lungs and heart. They spray too much and too often your tobacco."

"Well, Sheriff Sanchez, we got to keep the damn bugs off the crop. Why, if it weren't for the chemicals, those bugs would take over my entire plantation."

"Sí, Señor Manuel, but those chemicals will take out a few people. We know they cause cancer, and they're banned from the farms in the United States. That is why you come here to my country and ruin our land and exploit our people for low wages. Is that not true, Señor Manuel?"

"Look, Sheriff Sanchez, I'm not going to argue with you today, so just what the hell do you want with me?" asked Harry.

"Some of the workers are banding together and protesting about these foreign plantation owners, Señor Manuel, and they are mad about the low wages and those chemicals that the planes spray overhead when they are working," said the Sheriff.

"My people aren't complaining, and they get top wages for their work. So what are you trying to tell me this time, Sanchez?"

"No, no, no Señor Manuel. They do not complain about you. You are fair. But those other tobacco growers, they won't pay any higher wages, and they won't stop spraying their fields. The children are getting sick, and all the fish in our once-clear creeks are dying. . . ."

"That isn't my problem, Sanchez. I don't spray nearly as much as those other plantation owners, and you know it."

"Sí, but let me warn you, my friend. Those migrant workers are as mad as hell and they will not take much more."

"What are you saying, Sanchez?"

"They respect you. You are another shade of brown, and they like you. You are their friend and their brother. But shield yourself from those other plantation owners. Don't associate yourself with them, for those migrant workers will kill you when they come to kill those other owners who exploit them. That's all, my friend."

"Are you telling me that they plan on rebelling, Sanchez?"

"Sí, Señor. They told me to warn you and to tell you to shield yourself from those big business rip-off owners. You are an independent plantation owner, and you do not believe in slavery. But those other corporation owners, like Phillip Morris, have enslaved my people. They're sick and tired of it. They want their land and property back. They want their freedom. They will kill for their freedom, my friend."

"I hear you loud and clear, Sheriff Sanchez, and I won't associate myself with those other plantation owners. Thanks for the warning."

As the Venezuelan sheriff began to walk away, Harry thought to himself, there's something that man is trying to tell me, but he doesn't want to expose himself and perhaps damage his integrity. I know people, and from the expression of the sheriff's face, there's something wrong, or he wouldn't approach me with all that protection stuff that he'll give me if I don't join the other corporate owners.

Sanchez jumped in his Jeep and said, "One other thing, Señor Manuel. You will be approached by many other clans around this small and fruitful community. They will ask you to invest your money, time and talents into this revolution. Let them find their own sources and their own financing, Señor. Let them fight their own battles."

That was the message Harry (aka Manual) yearned for, those sweet words to his ears that Sheriff Sanchez was communicating in a roundabout way. Those words brought chills down his spine—invest, finance. It all spelled parlay. Why, that little Venezuelan must have found out he still had over six million dollars in his account after purchasing the tobacco farm and purchasing all the equipment for it in cash.

Sanchez was looking out for his people and looking out for himself. Harry figured Sanchez wanted him to invest in this so-called revolution, and he gave him a warning. Either go along with the plan or die. Well, he had news for that little Venezuelan. Nobody told Harry what to do and how to do it. He didn't live all those years being subservient to people like Sanchez, or to the big machines of the corporate world in Las Vegas.

But, come to think of it, it might not be such a bad idea. If he pitted one revolutionary faction against the other, he could reinvest his earnings in both sides and come out with a clear profit and more.

Maybe it wasn't worth it. He purchased this farm to retire and send all the dividends and profits for his children's and grandchildren's college education. And now this little Venezuelan wanted him to parlay his investment and talents into his revolutionary causes. No, not this time. He was tired of all this parlaying and he wanted to rest.

But it did sound intriguing. Not the money he'd make, but the pitting of two groups to make a substantial profit. He'd be respected by all the people in this country, as well as in the United States and Las Vegas. He went into the house to make a few phone calls and work out some of the logistics.

Phillip Morris was a corporate machine that exploited the low income people. Yeah, he thought, let me work out a scenario and get back with Sheriff Sanchez. This sounds intriguing. . . .

Back in Las Vegas, Sylvia and Thomas had found a new sensation, a new companion. The once athletically-built Thomas had, in two months' time, reduced his stature to resemble Woody Allen, just by pure association and the love that he had for Sylvia.

"Can you get some more, Babes?" Thomas said.

"Now, Thomas, quit looking on the floor and brushing the carpet to see if you dropped something. There's no cocaine down there. Do you realize you've been smoking this rock cocaine for the past month, and we've spent well over twenty-five thousand dollars?" Sylvia said as she lit up her base pipe and inhaled the last remaining piece of coke from the ounce that they'd just purchased last night.

"Oh, Babes, it really turns me on. I only want to do right by you. You know I love you, and we were supposed to be getting married, but I can't detach myself from that smoking. It's those drugs that give me such sensual and sexual feelings, and all I want to do is satisfy you."

"Satisfy me? How can you satisfy me when you can't even get an erection? You've smoked so much rock cocaine that you're sterile now. You've had a flat tire for the past month, and I've tried like hell to pump it up for you, but you just keep on smoking."

164

"Well, Babes," Thomas said, and his mouth began to salivate like one of Pavlov's dogs. His voice was incoherent. "You're the one who turned me on to the shit. And now you want to place me on the curve. I only did it for you."

"Cut it out with all that babes stuff and relax. Lay down for a few minutes. Your eyes are as wide and bulging as headlights on a diesel truck. You've had enough, Thomas."

"No, you're going to make another run and get some more right now. That money wasn't all yours. It was my money, too, so go back home and page the dope man and get another ounce," Thomas said in a hostile voice.

"No. You're crazy. You've had enough! Just look at you. You haven't eaten and you're shaking like a ten-point earthquake on the Richter Scale. Slow down and get some rest!"

"No, bitch! Don't tell me to slow down! You march your ass downstairs, get a cab and get some more money, or your ass is mine!"

"Fuck you, you white-looking, pale junkie!" Sylvia spat. She suddenly became nervous, seeing a different person in Thomas, a compulsive junkie and a violent maniac.

"Now, go right now and bring back another ounce!" Thomas yelled.

A terrible fight ensued, and glass and punches flew through the room. Sylvia tried to defend herself from his blows, to no avail. A hotel tenant heard the violent fight and called security, reporting that a rape was taking place.

"My brother will kill you! You just wait till he gets back. I'm going to tell him you tried to kill me," Sylvia said as the Security Police put a chokehold on Thomas and took him straight to jail.

"Your brother ain't shit, and nobody in your family is

worth a damn, bitch! I'm fed up with all those hustling-ass pimps, and that goes for your slot machine playing Mama," Thomas yelled out.

The party was over for Sylvia and Thomas. Sylvia had to go to the hospital for stitches for the blows that she suffered from the once-gentle man of her dreams, a boy who showed her a different way to live and a different avenue of life besides drugs. Now that same boy had become a compulsive drug junkie, attached to the drug cocaine, just for the love he had for Sylvia and wanting to satisfy her by any means possible.

Cocaine had turned that well-groomed and multi-talented, good-looking boy into a monster in a matter of a month and a half. Over thirty thousand dollars had been spent on this little fiasco that almost cost Sylvia her life.

It was all because of that feeling that smoking rock cocaine can give you. Once it reaches the threshold of the pleasure mechanisms of the brain, it makes you forget all other things in life. You can't identify with anything or anybody, and you're not able to see the fresh roses, let alone smell them. You're in your own little world, a zombie ready and willing to do anything to obtain a little more of that drug. Carjacking for the money? No problem, a cocaine junkie will do it. Automatic-teller-machine robbery? No problem, no sooner said than done, even if it means an outright murder for the ones who try to resist. No problem. They are all dead people. The junkie needs another blast to take him to the past. Forget about the future, for there is none . . . just that five-second rush. Over and over and over again.

* * *

"That son of a bitch!" Paula yelled after receiving

166

word from the hospital that Sylvia had been admitted, suffering from severe facial wounds and a broken arm and nose. "I'll kill that mother-fucker," she said as she hung up the phone and looked for Harry's number in the telephone book.

Where had she put that letter? Harry would have that bastard killed, whipping on her daughter. They were supposed to be getting married, and now look what had happened. It had to be those drugs. The last time she saw Thomas, he looked like he was losing a lot of weight. She was willing to bet that Sylvia had gotten that boy involved in her drug-taking.

Ah, here was Harry's number. She had to calm down and relax. Maybe it was Sylvia's own fault that she got her yellow ass whipped. She knew her daughter and her schemes. And if there was one thing she did know, when it came to using those drugs, Sylvia's whole personality changed. She'd sell her own baby just for more, or at least that's the way she was before they moved over here to Harry's house.

"Hello, may I please speak to Mr. Manuel?"

"Sí Señora. I will get Señor Manuel for you," the maid said politely with a Spanish accent.

"Hello, this is Caesar Manuel."

"Mr. Manuel, this is Mrs. Newman. How are you?"

"Paula, is that you?"

"Yeah, it's me. You caught onto the voice, and that's good."

"Yeah, and thanks for not exposing me on the phone. You know that these telephones down here are all two-party lines," said Harry.

"Sylvia is in the hospital. That no-good Thomas, the next-door neighbor doctor's son, beat her up. She's in serious condition."

"What? That doesn't sound like Thomas. What the hell happened, Paula?" Harry asked.

"Well, all I could get from the admissions clerk at the hospital is that Sylvia was whipped real bad by Thomas, and Thomas is in jail. They were both probably using those drugs. As a matter of fact, the money you gave Sylvia is almost all gone."

"She didn't buy a home?" Harry asked.

"No, all she bought is more of that drug and rented a room for a whole month near the Strip."

"Well, I'll be damned! Do you need me to come to Vegas and help in any way?"

"No, Harry. But that's not all the news. Harold Junior is in jail in Florida, and his bail is a hundred thousand dollars."

"Oh, Lord, what happened to Harold?" said Harry in distress.

"He got caught up in that drug trafficking, and Melinda left him and took most of his money. He called and left a message with me not to worry on the answer service, and said that he'll be home in a few days."

"Well, Harold is a man, and he can make a way for himself. He's had good training from the heavyweights, the hustlers. But I am concerned about Sylvia. What's her condition?"

"Serious now, Harry. But I'll go to the hospital this morning and find out how serious."

"Do that," Harry said, "and call me back as soon as possible. Paula, have you heard from any of the others in the gang?"

"Yeah," replied Paula. "Benny called and told me to give you his number."

"Okay, what is it? I'll call him and he can check things out with Sylvia for me."

"Here's the number—515-555-2345. Now, you call me back, Harry, and tell me what your plans are, and I'll go see Sylvia."

"Paula, tell Harold to keep his ass at home until I get there or call. You got me?"

"Okay, I got you. Bye."

Damn, thought Harry, that niece and nephew of mine are always screwing things up. Here they are, at the premium years of their lives, and can't do a damn thing right even if you give them over a quarter of a million dollars. They've botched that up already. I'll call Benny and find out who has the action on weapons on this side of the world.

He took a sip of his lemonade and dialed the phone. "Hello, Señor. Como esta? Esta Harry." He knew it was him, but knew from the oldest game in life, hustling and survival, that if you can't see them talking to you, always listen to the tone of voice before identifying yourself.

"Harry?" Benny asked.

"Yeah, amigo. How's the weather in San Mateo?"

"The crops are freezing over, amigo. My grapes are frostbit. Need I say more?"

"Will there be any wine this summer, my friend?"

"Sí, señor, but only if I hijack a French freighter, my friend."

"No sooner said than done," Harry responded, knowing that all the passwords were connected and answered decisively to identify Benny as Benny and Harry as Harry.

"Look, Ben, who has the action on the weapons down here? I got a few other things going on for myself than tobacco. Life got to be too boring, and once you relax and retire, you die."

"Sure, Harry. In Colombia, they're running guns and drugs. Your old pal, Smitty, he's got all the action on that sort of thing now."

"You mean Smiling Smitty, the one I had to break his jaw in a dispute over a poker game?"

"Yep, that's the one," Benny laughed. "Let me give you his number... here it is, 2-345-3847-457... some foreign number. Seems like a lot of numbers, but that's the way the telephone system is in the boondocks. Hey, let me give you my address so you can mail me that finder's fee."

"Yeah, Benny, do that. And to think, I thought you'd forgotten all about the Golden Rule of hustling, squeezing each other's palm for information given and received."

"Nope, I'm the one who wrote the book on it and established it for us old-time hustlers, sort of our retirement benefit package."

"Okay, Benny, it's in the mail."

"Call me back after you talk to Smitty. There are some things I want to discuss with you."

"Sure, I'll get right back with you."

Although there is no honor among thieves, Benny and Harry respected the game of hustling and always knew that once you were in the game, you were in the game for life.

Harry then called Smitty and talked to him about sending him a sample package of his "hardware," and discussed how he would disguise the package to look like a Central Intelligence Agency food relief package that would be dropped by a cargo plane.

"Good. A few 60-calibre machine guns might just come in handy around here on my plantation if what that sheriff is talking about is true. Either I'll sell the weapons to them or use those weapons on them. It doesn't make any difference to me whatsoever."

Harry had experienced his peak from that last sting,

and had lost all element for understanding the human need. He only thought about the money he would receive for running guns in this upcoming revolution. The thought never crossed his mind about how many innocent people would be killed and how many children would lose their parents in a revolt over the spraying of the tobacco fields. The chemical killed the bug pests, but it also, down the line, killed people.

Harry was beginning to think and act like a corporate manipulator, pitting one group against another just for the profit he could gain from doing wrong to his fellow man. Some call it capitalism, and others call it greed, but Harry went beyond that. After having that compulsive thrill of bringing down the big boys in Las Vegas, he now felt that the whole world would be at his disposal. Harry was becoming a compulsive maniac.

16

"Come on, amigo, the time is right for our escape," urged Jose as he and Harold switched uniforms with the Haitians. The Haitians were political prisoners, and weren't subjected to the same rules as the other prisoners, who'd committed crimes against the State. Political prisoners were allowed outside the jail cells for limited periods of time.

"My friend, the Haitians will shield us. Now, let's get moving!"

Harold and Jose slipped through the gate by holding their noses and getting down in the mud. The two then used their hands to dig as fast as possible to make their great escape while the Haitians clustered casually about them.

"Now, follow me, amigo. We must keep out of sight of the guards up on the tower. Stay close to me and we will both be free," said Jose as the two slipped and slid through the swamp, emerging where the lilies and alligators sat, eagerly awaiting their lunch. A Puerto Rican and an Afro-American would make a most tasty morsel for lunch, thought Harold, watching in terror as the cannibalistic creatures rushed for them.

"Come on, my friend, or you will be a sandwich for that creature approaching us! Jump into this little raft and we will be safe."

"Whoa! Thanks, Jose, you saved my life. That prehistoric monster almost took off my leg!"

"See, and he is chewing on my prison issued boot like it was chewing gum. I think we better get the hell out of here, and now."

Harold and Jose paddled the small raft downstream to freedom, trying to get their bearings. "That way, amigo, that way to the small road," urged Jose.

"The main road? If we go there, we'll be back inside that prison in minutes, you can bet on that!" said Harold.

"No, no, I made a few phone calls, and my señorita will be waiting for us. If she is not there, her Puerto Rican ass is mine. Now, keep moving, Harold, the road is straight ahead."

"There it is, right over there! Should we jump off the raft and swim the rest of the way?" Harold said anxiously.

"First we must check things out. The prison warden knows the only way out of that hellhole is through these swamps, and if we're not accounted for at lunch, the prison guards will be right there, waiting for the both of us, my friend. Let's hope that we were not detected as missing," Jose said.

Harold's heart began to pound faster and faster. "It's all because of that bitch, Melinda. She's the one who copped out on me."

"What was that?" asked Jose.

"Oh, nothing. I was just thinking about my girl and how she skipped out on me."

"Well, let us hope for your sake and mine that the money is in locker number twenty-three at the airport, and she did not take it," said Jose, keeping an eye on the road.

"Hey, how did you know about the locker number at the airport? You must be with the Feds, man. You're trying to set me up."

Harold took the heavy oak paddle and hit Jose

straight on the head with it, knocking him unconscious and then pushing him inside the small raft and sending it downstream.

"The warden or the alligators will be there to greet you, my friend, with my compliments." Harold then got on the road in the prone position, looking for a vehicle that could possibly be of any assistance to him. I knew things were too good to be true. Everything was perfect, too perfect. That water hole and the gate to slip through the fence, and the mud already dug for us. The raft. Only my Uncle Harry could have executed such a plan, not some stinking Puerto Rican Fed. They wanted to track me to see if I had any more drugs, any more kilos or cash. I better get moving before they find me.

Harold ran as fast as he could. He'd figured out one thing, and that was he'd never make it to the airport without being detected. He had to stage an accident here on the road to get one of those cars to stop.

Harold threw down some weeds on the road first, to get a passing motorist to slow down, and then he'd pretend like he was crossing the road. He'd hit the motorist's car's front fender with his fist as hard as possible and pretend like he was hit by the car. Here came a car now, and it was slowing down.

He ran across the street. The breaks screeched, and Harold hit the pavement. The driver was frantic and didn't know what to do.

"Oh, my God, look what I've done. I've killed this poor man!"

Harold groaned and moaned as if he were still alive, but hurt real bad. "My leg," Harold said. "Oh, my arm, my head. I think something's broken."

"Oh, my God. Let me wave down another motorist and get you to the hospital!"

"No, no time," Harold said as he moaned again.

"Well, then, I'll drive you to the hospital. Let's try to get you inside the car," said the lady. Judging from the scent of her perfume, she had money, Harold thought to himself. "Okay, now I'll take you to the nearest hospital," she said, still in a frenzy as she placed Harold's injured body in the back seat of her car.

Harold kept his eyes closed and his ears open as he lay on the back seat of her car. The seat was genuine leather. He could feel it and smell it. Harold tried to peek and find out how far the mysterious lady has driven so far. She had money. He could tell by her perfume and the car. Who was this mysterious woman?

"Don't worry, I'll have you at the hospital soon. What a lousy vacation this is turning out to be," she said to herself as Harold listened and tried to figure out what his next move was going to be.

"Going into shock," Harold said. "Must have water."

"Oh, my God!" exclaimed the lady. "I'll pull into this hotel and get help. I can't find a hospital."

"That's okay, just take me to the airport," Harold said, using his best manner.

She was startled. "I thought you were about to die, and now you seem fine. Is this a joke, or some of that car-jacking? Well, you can just take everything, but spare my life," she said. "It's just my luck." She began to cry. "First a divorce, and now a car-jacking. It wasn't enough that that attorney tried to take me for everything. And that good-for-nothing husband. My father tried to tell me about him, but I was in love."

"Lady, calm down. I'm not going to harm you or take your car. Just take me to the International Airport and drop me off there as soon as you can."

"You mean you're not going to rob me?"

175

"No, ma'am. Do I look like a robber?"

"Well, no, but who can distinguish a robber these days? Everybody is so crazy now."

"I'm not a robber. I'm an escaped prisoner," he laughed.

"Oh, my God," she yelled. "You're going to kill me!"

"No," Harold said, "I was set up and put in jail. They took my brand new 5.0 Mustang that my uncle bought me and all of my money. I was framed."

"You expect me to believe that? Oh, please don't kill me."

"Look, lady, my nails are manicured, and if you can see through all of this mud, look at this detailed Number 1 Rap haircut. Supercuts don't give these kind of haircuts to prisoners. Now do you believe me?"

"Well, I don't know. It's so hard to trust anyone these days, especially men."

Harold then climbed over to the front seat as the lady kept driving. "Look at me," Harold said. "I'm as helpless as a kitten up a tree, not knowing my right foot from my left."

She started laughing so hard she started to cry. "Well, anybody with that kind of sense of humor deserves a ride to the airport. I can trust you, can't I?"

"Yes, you can trust me."

The two drove a few more miles and then a conversation began.

"What's your name?" she asked.

"My name is Harold, what's yours?"

"My name is Cynthia."

"Cynthia? My little niece is named Cynthia. Good to meet you."

"Tell me, Harold, how in the world did you escape from the prison you were in?"

"I slid through the gate," Harold said, and Cynthia began to laugh.

"You can't go to the airport looking like that. They'll find you, and then you'll be right back in prison. I'll stop at the next hotel and you'll be able to take a shower and get some other clothes."

"Lady, I mean Cynthia, I have no money or identification. All my money is at the airport," Harold said sadly.

"Well, I can loan you the money until you get to the airport, and then you can repay me. Deal?"

"It's a deal. Cynthia, I know it's none of my business, but where did you get the cash to purchase this new Mercedes Benz?"

"When I graduated from Yale my father bought it for me. It's a graduation gift. My dad threatened to take it away from me if I married that bum I was married to. I let him have it, and then I found out what a creep that Stanley, my annulled husband, was. I got rid of him and got my car back."

"Well, you made the right move, lady. This car is bad."

"There's a Comfort Inn. You can take a shower there and I'll try to find you some clothes in town. I'll give you some money to take a cab to the airport and give you my address so you can mail me the money. Is that an agreement, Harold?"

"Sure, Cynthia. And thanks for trusting me."

At the motel, she said, "You stay down and I'll get the room. If they see you in those clothes, they'll surely put you back in jail."

Cynthia went to the registration desk and got a room on the bottom floor.

The hotel attendant was nosy and looked at the nice car. "That's a room with two queen beds, ma'am."

"Yes. My husband is taking care of our luggage."

"Very well, ma'am. Room 127. I hope you and your husband enjoy your stay."

"Thank you," replied Cynthia as she took the key and went to open the room.

"Whew. Look at the ham hocks on her! She was taken care of real well. And that smile, those teeth, that tall, slender body . . . I'd give a toss to the fool who let her go," muttered the attendant.

Inside the room, Cynthia called out quietly, trying to get Harold's attention. "Harold, come on, the room is open."

Harold jumped out and hurried into the room, bringing a cloud of dirt and mud inside with him.

"My, you are dirty, aren't you," Cynthia remarked.

"I'll send some money to clean your car up, too. It's a mess," said Harold.

"That's okay, Harold. Listen, I have to make a few phone calls. You don't mind if I stay here while you take your shower, do you?"

"No, not at all, Cyn."

"Cyn, you called me Cyn. How did you know that was my nickname?"

"Oh, that's what we call my little niece."

"That's funny. Okay, here's your key, and the shower's right through there."

"Thanks. What should I do with these filthy clothes? And what about the clothes I'll wear out of here?"

"Just let me call my parents. They expected me to call a long time ago. Then I'll run down to the nearest Kmart and pick you up a few things."

"Kmart? Try stopping at Neiman Marcus instead, Cyn. Besides, you're going to get the money back anyway, right?"

"Well, I guess you're right. Okay, Neiman Marcus. What are your sizes?"

"Here, I'll write it all down on this pad."

"Okay. I'll use the phone and be right back while you're soaking."

Harold took a good hot shower. The room was all steamed up when he finished. He didn't expect Cynthia to still be in the main room, and he came out of the shower wearing just a towel.

"Oh, excuse me. I thought you were gone," he said.

Cynthia looked at Harold and his strong body and dropped the phone. Her mouth hung open as she kept looking at his muscled torso and body. The phone was on the floor, and her mother was still talking, but she just kept looking at Harold.

"Uh, Cynthia, don't you want to pick up the phone? Your mother might be worried."

"Oh, yeah. Call you back, Mother." She hung up abruptly. "I wasn't expecting you to come out of the room right then, at least not like that," Cynthia said as she gazed at Harold's chest and body.

"Sorry, you have to excuse me. I thought you were gone shopping."

"Not yet; you see, my mother, she's always worried about me. I just talked a little too long. Harold," she continued in a soft voice, "do you have a girlfriend?"

"I had one, but I'm footloose and fancy free now," he responded.

"I was just wondering. You see, I never had an Afro-American boyfriend, and I've always heard such kinky things about Black boys in college. Now don't get me wrong, we're just friends, right?"

"Yeah, Cyn, just friends."

"But I just couldn't help but notice your masculine

179

body. You look like a body builder."

"Why, thank you. But if you don't get me those clothes, I'll be a dead man from pneumonia."

"Oh, I'm so sorry. I'll go take care of that right now. Matter of fact, my ex-husband left some of his clothes in my car. He wasn't as muscular as you are, but his clothes are all designer label."

"That would be great. And then you can get back on the road before it gets too late. You know all about how accidents happen late at night. The road out there is so dangerous," Harold said.

"Yeah, I guess I'd better get going."

Maybe they had the same idea and said it at the same time. "If it's all right with you, I'd like to stay the night. I'm kind of tired, too tired to drive any more."

Harold looked at her. "That's fine with me. After all, you paid for the room. We'll go Dutch."

"Now, no funny stuff."

"Of course not, Cynthia. I'm not that kind of guy."

"Good. Then it's agreed. You stay in that bed, and I'll sleep in this one. Let's shake on it." Cynthia went out to the car to get the other bag and the clothes, and when she returned, Harold was inside the covers, sound asleep with his light on. He was sleeping in the nude.

Cynthia began biting her nails and trying to figure out a way to get next to Harold without it being too obvious. Why did she have such strong sexual urges? She wanted to climb in that bed with him, but she didn't want to offend him. Oh well, she wasn't ashamed of her body, and he certainly wasn't ashamed of his. And she was needing a man. Her ex-husband wasn't much in that department.

Cynthia took off her clothes and slipped into bed with Harold. Feeling her warmth next to him, he rolled over and took her into his arms, saying, "What took you so long?"

They began to laugh and caress each other, and Cynthia reached over and turned out the light.

*   *   *

Paula hurried into the hospital and rushed to the intensive care ward. Was that Sylvia, with an I.V. in her arm? That goddamned boy tried to kill her!

"Sylvia, it's me, your mama. Can you hear me?"

"Yeah, Mom, I hear you and see you. I was asleep after they gave me those drugs to ease the pain."

"Just look at you. Your nose is taped up and your eyes are black! What happened to you, Sylvia? You two were so much in love."

"I still love him, Mother. It was all my fault. I'm the one who got Thomas on those drugs. It was my fault and my desire to have those drugs, and now I'm paying for it."

"Didn't I tell you that those drugs, smoking that cocaine, would get you killed?"

"Yeah, Mama, you told me. But cocaine is like a magnetic attraction. Once you've had it one time, you'll always want more. One hit off that pipe isn't enough, and two hits is too many. This time I learned, and learned the hard way. Never again in my life will I use those drugs. I'm ready to go into therapy."

"Yes, child, we're all ready to seek professional help for our compulsive behaviors, whether it's using drugs, dealing them, or playing the slots. It's all the same, and they affect you the same way. All three things will bring you down to another level in life."

"I know it, but I love Thomas and only wish I had him back."

"Sylvia, I talked to Thomas's father. He went to bail Thomas out of jail, since you didn't press charges. The

181

damages will be paid for with your remaining money."

"Take the money, Mother, take all of it. I don't want it. That money has done nothing but evil things to me and my lover. I'm through with all these games. Keep me out of Uncle Harry's affairs."

"Sylvia, your brother Harold is in jail and has lost all his money, so I think you're right. All money is not good money. Let's start a new life with the money I have left. We have to stop our ways and come down to earth. We have to deal with the realities of life and stick to living the natural way, not life in the fast lane. Maybe it just wasn't meant for us to have all the nice things in life. Although we were poor, we were happier living in the housing projects. Now, I'm not saying we have to move back, but we can buy a place we can afford and live where we are accepted. That's all we need. It'll work out for us as long as we're together."

"Okay, Mother, whatever you say. Right now, I'm tired and I need to rest."

"All right, sweetheart. I'll visit you later." Paula kissed her daughter one more time and left the ward. She began to think of what Sylvia had said about that money and it being jinxed. She was probably right. That parlay shit ruined her whole family—Harold was in jail and Sylvia was in intensive care in the hospital.

That damned Harry. While he was puffing on a cigar and cooling it in the shade, she was worried to death about her kids. That was his whole parlay plan—to ruin them so he could use the investments from them. He just used them to boost his excessive ego trip. Well, she would call him and give him a piece of her mind!

17

His shipments had been coming in as planned and on schedule. Harry uncrated another box of weapons. Now he had enough weapons to approach that little Venezuelan cop and show him he was ready to deal with his people. Then he'd approach the other revolutionaries, then meet with the oppressors, and that all added up to a perfect parlay of investments, which spelled *money*.

He went back to the house. He had to get more money wired to Smitty and tell him to keep those weapons coming. He had too much invested in this now, and it was too late to turn around.

Harry defined the whole meaning of the parlay ethic by first selling sixty-millimeter machine guns to the guerilla groups who were hiding in the hills and making small hits on the powerful corporate machines that were protected by the Venezuelan government. The corporations were supported by the United States through funding to keep those tobacco farms growing, farms that produced those cancer sticks that the Americans and Canadians craved in the compulsion for a quick charge of nicotine.

Next, Harry made an agreement with Sheriff Sanchez's group, which was looked upon by the Venezuelan government and the United States government as peace keeping. Both governments funded the brigades of now-Captain Sanchez with millions of dollars; Sanchez's group purchased 60-millimeter machine guns and grenade launchers from Señor Caesar Manuel.

The tobacco companies like Philip Morris funded Harry with millions of dollars for the necessary protection they needed to pacify the natives and keep the rebellions at bay.

Harry had discovered the perfect gamble since the Mirage robbery, and it was safe and secure. His profits soared, and his compulsive behavior ran neck to neck with them like two horses in a photo finish. But only one could win.

In his letters, Paula could read between the lines. Harry had become too greedy and had lost all fear of taking any risk. All he wrote about was the money he was making and how he pitted his one-time neighbors, friends, and relatives against each other, as if they were bulldogs in a deadly fight for the same turf. Harry had parlayed the shit out of those four factions, in a bet that one group or the other would need his hardware and weapons before he needed them. They all called upon Caesar Manuel to literally kill each other in a cold and miscalculated revolution.

"Mr. Manuel . . . or can I call you Caesar?" Mr. Daniels, the representative from Philip Morris was there to get information on how the revolution was going and also to make sure his own tobacco farms were safe and secure. "It looks like right over that hill there has been an explosion," the PR rep said.

"Yeah, we get those every now and then," Harry said as he lit a large cigar.

"Are we in any immediate danger here?"

"No, not unless I talk on this two-way radio and tell them we have a few renegades right here on my farm."

"I hope that isn't the case, Caesar," laughed Daniels.

"Well, it's like this. If that briefcase you're carrying doesn't have my profit-sharing money in it, I'll just call and tell them there are renegades here on the property, and there might be a few fireworks . . . with you in the middle of them."

"Here you are, Mr. Manuel. You'll find the regular amount inside that briefcase, just what the other plantation owners have agreed upon."

"That's fine. Now I'll have one of my men escort you out, Mr. Daniels," said Harry.

"That won't be necessary. I was driven here in that Range Rover over there. It's one of the company's trucks."

"No . . . it's now my truck," said Harry. "Just think of it as a loss to your company, Mr. Daniels. Besides, you would never have gotten out of here alive, driving that vehicle, so you might as well leave it here."

"If that's what you want, Mr. Daniels. We'll fax you the papers . . . that is, if I get back to the Philip Morris corporate office safe and sound."

"Like I said, one of my men will escort you to my airfield, and then you can leave in one piece. My pilot will fly you outside the battle zone."

"Thank you, Mr. Manuel. It was a pleasure doing business with you."

"The pleasure is mine," said Harry. "Oh, by the way, at the next stockholders' meeting, relay the message that my vote and my shares have a substantial say-so on the decisions about sabotaging that other cigarette company, so when the tally is made, don't forget me next time."

"Yes, sir, I'll relay the message," said Daniels as he jumped into the jeep.

"Next time, take one of the corporate jets," Harry said and laughed. "I need a new aircraft."

*   *   *

Paula was looking at the pictures that Harry had just sent her. "This is ridiculous. He's gone crazy and thinks he's some slave master now, with all those poor people relying on him to distribute food and provide shelter for them."

Harry's tobacco plantation had begun to take on a new aspect. It looked like a Southern plantation during the old slave trade era in the United States. The migrant tobacco workers were housed in different sections of the farm in trailers, while guests and dignitaries stayed in the main house, which had been remodeled to look like a mansion out of *Gone With the Wind*.

"Look at this picture, Sylvia." Paula showed her a picture of Harry in all white, wearing an old Confederate hat and smoking a long cigar.

"Uncle Harry must think he's Rhett Butler or something," Sylvia laughed, handing the pictures back to her mother. She winced, feeling a pain in her side where her ribs were broken from her altercation with Thomas.

"Honey, you just lie down and I'll fix your lunch. Uncle Harry has really cracked up, child. Just think, after all those years that our people were slaves and in bondage, and now he turns around and does the same thing to those poor, unfortunate Venezuelan migrant workers. Harry's using them as slaves for his own wealth and greed, and for the satisfaction of controlling people."

"Mama, Uncle Harry used to tell us he was the descendant of President Thomas Jefferson. Didn't

186

Thomas Jefferson have slaves?"

"Yes, but from what I read in history, Thomas Jefferson treated his slaves like people, not animals, and he courted several of the Negro women and impregnated them."

"Come on now, Mother, you can never treat a slave like a person. They're told what to do and how to do it, and then are locked up like animals. Those history books are always in favor of the powerful people, and never tell the true story."

"I know, Sylvia. You're right about that. Whenever money is involved, things get turned in favor of those who have rather than those who have not."

"Speaking of being locked up like animals, have you heard from Harold?"

"Oh, let me tell you, honey, Harold got out of jail and is now living in Hartford, Connecticut, with his new girlfriend. I didn't want to tell you while you were in the hospital, knowing that you wanted to see your big brother and would be disappointed."

"Who is it this time, Mother? Don't those people in Hartford got a lot going for themselves?"

"Yes, honey. Harold called and told me that his new girlfriend's family is part of the blue-blood society there, and have plenty of money. Cynthia's family is kind of like the Duponts and Rothchilds."

"That's a strange thing in our society, Mama. The super rich people don't care what color you are. They accept you for your character. But poor people are always complaining that either you have more than they do or you don't deserve certain things in life. They're jealous and envious," Sylvia said.

*   *   *

187

When Harold and Cynthia met on that strange night when Harold faked a car injury, Harold was at first using Cynthia, who was naive and gullible. But that gullibility and innocence were the necessary ingredients for the two lovers, who had become inseparable.

Harold and Cynthia were at her parents' house in Hartford, enjoying each other's company. "You know, Harold," Cynthia said, "my father doesn't even know what you are."

"What you do mean, Cyn?" Harold asked, looking completely surprised at her comment.

"Well, he doesn't know if you are Afro-American, since you're so light-skinned, even though you have such curly hair. And Mother treats you as if you were her son."

"Cyn, sometimes I wish the whole world had insight like your parents and didn't look at people in a purely negative way just because of their color. Your mother and father are swell people, and I love them dearly, but when that baby gets here, they'll find out what nationality I am, and that's for damn sure," Harold said. He laughed and walked up to her and felt her stomach, trying to communicate with his unborn child.

"My parents are caught up in that corporate money-making world, Harold. I've been trying to get them to take a vacation, but instead of them taking time off, they bring the vacation to them."

"Yeah, who needs a vacation when all you have to do is get on that sixty-five foot yacht that's parked in your own back yard? I'll be glad when I finish that navigational school your father's sending me to. Then I'll be able to command that baby."

"You can commandeer me any time, sweetheart." Cynthia and Harold melted into each other's arms, then turned and went quickly upstairs to their bedroom in the guest quarters of her parents' estate to make love. It was something they did every time something sweet was said. That old magical and mystical urge called love pointed its arrow in their direction frequently. They were both completely happy with each other and communicated with each other effectively, even though they were complete different backgrounds—one highly wealthy and born into a fortune, the other very poor and born into poverty and deprivation. But love conquers all extremes.

* * *

"Mother, mother!" Sylvia called out from her sickbed. "Thomas just called and said that Uncle Harry's picture is in the *Fortune 500* magazine as being one of the most successful businessmen in the world, with prospects of being one of the richest."

"What? Why, that damned fool! Don't he know that he'll be exposed and bring on the heat? They investigate those people, and when those tabloids get ahold of the story, we may all be in San Quentin! I'm going to phone him right now and tell Harry he'd better quit while he's ahead."

As Paula called, she could feel the sudden pressure and the pain of what Harry had caused and repeatedly told herself that it wasn't worth it, it just wasn't worth it. Not a damn bit of it.

"Yes, may I speak to Mr. Caesar Manuel, please?"

"May I ask who is calling?"

"This is his sister-in-law, Paula. Now put him on the phone," Paula said in an angry manner. That fool, Harry, had a new butler with an English accent, she thought to herself. He really does think he's some kind of an aristocrat, and now she knew she was going to have to fly down to Venezuela to straighten him out.

Caesar Manuel picked up the phone, and before he could even say a word, he could hear Paula yelling and ranting about his tyrant ways. Harry interrupted her, "Is that you, Paula?"

"Harry Simmons, what the hell are you doing down there? Do you know that your picture and plantation are in the *Fortune 500* magazine? You're considered to be one of the prospective richest men in the whole world."

"Isn't that great, Paula?" Harry said, as Paula listened in complete disbelief.

"Now I know you've lost your cotton-pickin' mind! Don't you know that the FBI will see you in that magazine and come down there and serve you with extradition papers?"

"Look, Paula, don't worry about what I'm doing down here. I have a business to run and I'm doing a good job at it. You just worry about taking care of the baby and Sylvia, and I will finance the rest."

"You're nuts and you're a user and a tyrant, Harry. The very things that you've always been against. Remember—you always fought against the big corporate machines of Las Vegas. I distinctly remember hearing you say, 'They didn't give me the chance in life that I deserved because I am Afro-American.' Those very same things that you were against, and now look at you. You're part of it. Slavery at its finest, and the complete exploitation of the poor and deprived people," Paula said angrily, and she began to cry.

"Let me tell you something, Paula. I'm doing this for the family. We are part of a dynasty now. We finally made it, and it's time that we take our rightful place in life and retain our resources and make them grow. If you can't understand that, girl, there's something wrong with you."

190

Paula slammed the phone down. That fool. I know what I'll do, she thought. I'm flying down there to Venezuela to convince that fool that it's time to face the realities of the real world before it's too late.

"Sylvia, I'll call the hospital and hire a nurse to take care of you and the baby. I'm going on a trip to South America."

"Don't bother, Mother. Thomas will take care of us while you're visiting Uncle Harry," Sylvia said in a low voice and with a sinful smile.

"Thomas? You mean to tell me that Thomas and you are back together after the way he almost killed you? Are you crazy? This whole family has gone completely nuts! It's time for me to take some time off before they commit me to the mental institution! I'm calling the airport right now and you, Sylvia, with your dumb, nymphomaniac self, you call your Uncle Harry and tell him I'm on my way. Remember, Sylvia, if I hear that you and Thomas are using those drugs inside this house, I'm calling the police on both of you. Is that understood?"

"Yes, Mother. And, Mom, thanks for allowing Thomas back in the house. I love you, Mom," she said as Sylvia dialed the airport.

As she packed, Paula shouted, "Honey, don't you know that I knew a long time ago that Thomas has been climbing through your bedroom window at night? Don't you know that this house has an alarm on each and every window, child?"

"Alarm on every window?" Sylvia said in surprise.

"Yes, and every time that boy climbed through the window, I woke up and turned the silent alarm off. When he left in the morning, I turned it back on."

"You knew all the time, didn't you, Mother?"

"Yes, I knew, but I didn't do anything about it, because

one thing I've learned in life, and that is you can't fight the power of love. Sylvia, did you reach your Uncle Harry?"

"I'm trying to call him right now. Don't forget I'm still immobile in this bed."

"Well, you were pretty mobile the other night when that boy from next door climbed through the window. You're going to have to make other arrangements for your secret love rendezvous. I'm not running a motel here," Paula said jokingly.

"Oh, Mother. As soon as I get well, I'm going to search for a good man for you. That's what you need in your life, a man to give you that afterglow. You need a sex life."

"Child, you just stay out of my business. I told you and Harold years ago the only man that would ever be in my life is and was your father. I ain't got no time for fooling around at my age. Come to think of it, maybe Harold can go with me to that foreign country. After all, a male figure to accompany me may be necessary. No telling what the hell your Uncle Harry has gotten himself into. I'll call your brother right now."

Paula was nervous and anxious to get down to that plantation and give her brother-in-law a few choice words of advice, and try to convince him to leave well enough alone. He had to get out of the racketeering world once and for all.

"Yes, may I speak to Harold Simmons?" Paula said.

"Is this Mrs. Simmons," asked Cynthia.

"Yes, and how are you doing, Cynthia?" Paula responded with a cheerful grin.

"Oh, we're fine, Mrs. Simmons. We're looking forward to visiting you next month."

"Well, honey, both of you may have to come and visit sooner than I had originally planned."

"What? Is there a problem, Mrs. Simmons?"

"Girl, that uncle of Harold's needs us, and he's way down in Venezuela."

"That's what Harold was telling us. He has a tobacco farm down there, doesn't he?"

"Tobacco farm ain't the word, it's a tobacco plantation."

"Well, here's Harold. If there's anything that I or my family can do, please let us know."

"Thank you, dear," said Paula. She continued to listen through the phone as Cynthia talked to Harold.

"Harold, put your pants on, it's your mother on the phone."

"How is she going to see me naked through the phone? She's way in Las Vegas," said Harold as he slipped on his pants.

"Hello, Mom."

"Harold Junior, have you been screwing again?" Paula said in a loud voice. "Boy, what're you trying to do, have twins or maybe quadruplets? Boy, I'm telling you, you never give that thing of yours a chance to rest. Every time I call, you and Cynthia are just getting out of bed, just getting out of the shower, just getting out of the spa," Paula said jokingly.

"Hey, when I didn't have no one, you accused me of being gay, and now you're accusing me of being oversexed. What is a man to do?"

"Nothing, just nothing, but keep that thing of yours zipped up or buttoned up before you damage my grandbaby in Cynthia's stomach," said Paula with a laugh.

"Mother! I am appalled! Now what's this I've been hearing about Uncle Harry? I told Sylvia about that article. What's going on with him and that tobacco plantation he has in Venezuela?"

"Harold, I want to ask you a favor. I have to get down

193

there and talk to your uncle. He's getting too deep into what he's doing down there. I want to know if you can go down there with me."

"Why, sure. You know damn well I'd do anything for Uncle Harry."

"You better ask your wife, first," said Paula.

"Mother, you know we haven't set a date on marriage yet."

"Well, you might as well get married; you're getting all of the benefits already."

"Mother! Besides, she'd coming along with us," said Harold.

"Good. I'll make reservations for us, and you call me back as soon as possible."

"Okay, Mom. Wait just a second, Cynthia is trying to tell me something." He covered the phone with his hand and Paula could hear a muffled conversation taking place. "Okay, sweetheart. I'll tell her. Cynthia said that when her father arrives home, she'll convince her parents it's time for them to meet you and the rest of the family. She's going to get her parents to take that trip with us to Venezuela."

"Great! I'll wait until I hear from you before I make the reservations," Paula said with a sigh of relief.

"Oh, and Mother, if Cynthia can convince her parents to take that overdue vacation, they will be taking their private Lear jet, so we'll make all the plans for the travel arrangements."

"Sure, son. Call me tonight to let me know. Bye, sweetheart."

"Bye, Mother. And Cynthia said she looks forward to meeting you."

"Give her and her family my love."

"Okay. Talk to you soon."

Paula called out to the next room. "Sylvia. Sylvia!"

"What is it now? I'm trying to get some rest," Sylvia said, attempting to open her eyes.

"Rest? Honey, you better try to get some exercise. You're getting fat again, and those bones of yours aren't going to heal right unless you exercise them. Oh, that's right. You get plenty of exercise at night when Thomas comes crawling through your window."

"Mother, you're always accusing me of something," said Sylvia, and she tried to roll over again to catch a few more winks.

"Your brother may be coming to visit with his wife and her family. They'll be calling back this afternoon to let us know."

"Harold is married now?"

"Well, you could say he is. Cynthia is having his baby, and they're making the wedding arrangements now," Paula said.

"Well, Barbara had his baby, and he didn't marry her," Sylvia replied sarcastically.

"Don't be so negative. I think your brother really loves this girl."

"Sure. As soon as I hear the wedding bells, I'll believe it. Cynthia is Caucasian, isn't she?"

"Yes, not that it makes a difference. You're close to being white yourself, and as soon as Thomas and you have any children, that batch of genes and melon will be white or another shade of brown all over again. Your grandfather was a white man, and Thomas's father, the surgeon, is half-white. So what are you saying, Sylvia?"

"Nothing, Mother, nothing at all. Just let me get some rest."

195

"Did you call your Uncle Harry and tell him that I'm coming to see him?"

"Yes, and he said he'll be expecting you. Now, I need a nap."

"Okay, child. You rest up while I cook and try to plan dinner and go shopping for our expected guests."

18

Harold and Cynthia and her parents arrived in Las Vegas that Friday morning on a hot and smothering day. A private limousine picked them up at Mr. Hunter's corporate Lear jet at the airport.

"Wow, it's certainly hot here in Las Vegas," remarked the billionaire heir to the famous and philanthropic family fortune. "How did you manage to live here, Harold, with this incredible desert heat?"

"After living here for so long, Mr. Hunter, you adjust to the climate. It's taken me more than three months to adjust to the climate in Connecticut," Harold said as he helped the limo driver load the luggage in the trunk of the car. "Is this your first time in Las Vegas, Mr. Hunter?"

"Oh no, son. We have investments right here in Las Vegas. I'm one of the major shareholders of the Mirage Hotel and Casino."

Harold almost fainted and thought to himself, this certainly is a small and strange world. Here I am, engaged to be married to the girl I love so dearly, and I was in on the biggest robbery in the history of the world, and it was one of Cynthia's father's major stock investments. It could only happen in America!

The limousine driver drove off the runway and headed up toward Highway 15, where he went south past the Excaliber Hotel and Casino and viewed the partially-constructed new MGM Hotel and Casino.

"Every time I come back to Las Vegas, they add something new. Look at that. That old Dunes Hotel and Casino is now owned by our corporation. I think the water park that will be built there will attract quite a few people, don't you, Harold?"

"I don't think I want to comment on that, Mr. Hunter." Harold shied away from that question. Only Cynthia and he knew the reason. Cynthia knew the whole story about everything that went down in Las Vegas almost a year ago. Now she looked at her man, hugged him, and changed the subject. The limo merged to the right and got off the freeway on Sahara, where the Simmons estate was.

"This is a lovely neighborhood, honey. Why don't we purchase a home here in Vegas? That way we can see the shows and entertain here," Mrs. Hunter said to her husband.

Harold sunk down even deeper in his seat, knowing that Vegas could break the best of the billionaires with its subliminal suggestive devices that were used to lure the people into those casinos.

"What's wrong, Harold? Are you getting carsick?" Mr. Hunter asked.

"Nothing, sir. Well, maybe there is something. I've told Cynthia what kind of place Las Vegas really is, and I'll tell you, too. Vegas is not a place for a family, Mr. Hunter."

"What do you mean? I always thought that Las Vegas was family oriented."

"No, sir. This is the worst place to raise a family. The scum of the earth live right here in this city."

"What!" Mr. and Mrs. Hunter looked at each other in total surprise. "Well, Harold, as soon as we get settled, we'll talk about the problems that this city has and why it isn't a good place to raise a family. From the Board Meetings, I know the population has increased dramatically in this city, and there are plenty of opportunities for young people to get started in life."

"Yes, sir, and there are also some subliminal elements that you cannot see. But they exist," Harold said as he stretched out and stuck out his chest and tried to explain to Mr. Hunter about those suggestive and all-so-powerful signals that are sent to the naive and unfortunate people who visit for the first time. Some never left again, due to the suggestive mechanisms rigged up in all of the casinos and motels.

As the driver pulled up at the Simmons estate, Mr. Hunter was both surprised and amazed at what Harold was saying. Being an astute and very clever business-man, he knew that if these subliminal suggestive powers could turn a person on, there could be a mechanism devised to turn a person off. Mr. Hunter only looked at the whole thing from a business point of view.

"Harold," he said as the four were about to get out of the limo and approach the front door, "I'm going to call my research and development lab and have some of my research assistants find out everything possible about subliminal suggestive powers from the time an infant is in the crib with the lullaby to the time when that same grown-up person goes to play that first slot machine."

Inside the house, Harold introduced his mother to Mr. and Mrs. Hunter and Cynthia. Sylvia was in her room with Thomas. The Hunters thought that they would have the opportunity to meet Sylvia and her boyfriend the next morning. The maid escorted the Hunters to their rooms in the guest house, while Harold and Cynthia talked for a lit-tle while longer to Paula.

"You have a beautiful home, Mrs. Simmons."

"Why, thank you, Cynthia. It originally belonged to my

199

brother-in-law, and he claimed it over to us," said Paula as the two sat down in the living room, sipping a cup of tea.

"Mrs. Simmons, I just want to tell you how much I appreciate how your family accepted my family and tell you how much I love your son, Harold. He's so good to me, and my parents just adore him."

"Yes, child, Harold has certainly matured over the years. Two years ago, you couldn't even talk to him. He was just like a stone wall, and nobody could tell him a thing."

"Oh, Harold and I talk about everything. And we have some good news for you."

"What else is there, child? The baby is on its way and you two will be married in a few weeks. Is there any other things that I should know?" Paula asked.

"Yes, we're having twins! Harold and I decided to name them, if they're boys, Harold and Harry."

Paula fainted, and the maid and Harold had to revive her.

The next morning, the Hunters were having breakfast as Mr. Hunter called back to Bridgeport, Connecticut, where his headquarters were located.

"What I need is some data on subliminal suggestive powers and some of that brainwashing literature. Research anything you can find out about gratification and compulsive behavior as it relates to gambling. I'll be back in the office next Friday."

"Yes, sir. I'll have all that material on your desk when you return," the technician said.

Mr. Hunter hung up the phone and then called his private pilot to get a flight scheduled for today for the trip to Venezuela. Mr. Hunter had ulterior motives in researching the subject of compulsive behavior and persistent gambling. After all, he was a major stockholder and had over thirty-nine percent of stocks in the Mirage Corporation.

"The limousine has arrived," he called out. "Let's load up!" He said goodbye to Sylvia and told her to get as much therapy as possible to get those bones strong so she could come visit that summer for Harold and Cynthia's wedding. Mrs. Hunter gave Sylvia a big hug and then got into the limousine along with Harold, Cynthia and Paula.

Harold said, "I can't wait to see Uncle Harry."

"Son, there are a few things I'd like to tell you and the Hunters before we get there. Harry has changed a great deal. First of all, he's changed his name to Caesar Manuel."

"Caesar Manuel? I've read a lot about Caesar Manuel and his overnight success in the tobacco industry," said Mr. Hunter.

The limousine driver brought them up to the plane, which had been cleared to take off.

"You know, we once had investments in the tobacco industry, but we voted to relinquish our stocks, since it was discovered that second-hand smoke causes cancer. Also, the tobacco industry has been involved with spraying heavy pesticides on those tobacco crops."

"Mr. and Mrs. Hunter, I really appreciate you going out of your way to take us to Venezuela. You just don't know how much this means to me."

"Any time, Paula. Any time you and your family would like to charter a flight, just call the corporate office and they will accommodate you. Harold is my son, also, Paula, and he has shown me a new look at life. We're putting together a package that will address the environment and will help in minority hiring and training. I was so hung up on the business I never had time to smell the roses, and now Harold and I go yachting and fly fishing. He's given me another outlook on life."

The flight was all smooth sailing, and soon the six-passenger Lear jet landed at the Venezuelan International Airport. The Hunters decided to stay at the Venezuelan Hilton Hotel and Casino while Harold, Cynthia and Paula set off on a mission of mercy to convince Harry, the so-called King of the Crossroaders, to come back to the United States to live and face the music for all his wrong-doings. It was never too late to start a new life, free from performing devious and heinous crimes against one's fellow man.

Harry's driver was there at the airport, waving a sign indicating "The Manuel Guests" as they entered the gate and Customs checked out their passports and other identification needed to enter the country. The heat and humidity were hard to bear as they were escorted to the truck where the driver was waiting. The luggage was secured on top of the Range Rover.

The Hunters went directly to their hotel room on a second honeymoon, and the other three started straight out to Mr. Caesar Manuel's tobacco plantation with the air conditioning on full blast.

"Mother, look at this beautiful countryside. Now I know why Uncle Harry chose this place to retire. Everything is so green and tropical," Harold said as the driver pointed out a few historical sites.

"Yes, it does look beautiful," Paula agreed. "But, knowing your Uncle Harry, he hasn't got the time or the patience to smell the roses, or whatever those kinds of flowers are over there. He's too busy counting money day in and day out."

"Well, Cynthia and I wouldn't mind living here and raising our children, not having to worry about the violence that's happening in the United States. Would we, babes?" Harold leaned over and placed his hands on Cynthia's stomach and listened for a heartbeat.

Paula thought, just look at him. Lord, those two better be praying that what's inside Cynthia's stomach ain't no twin boys. If they only had to go through half of the things I had to with Harold Senior, their father, and Harry, their uncle, they would have changed their minds a long time ago and realized they were just having a real bad nightmare. If it weren't for those counselors and psychiatrists that she'd been seeing over the last year, she felt she'd have been institutionalized a long time ago.

Sometimes people had to rely on professional therapy for their problems. That was why those doctors went to school for all those years—to be able to help people. Most minority people didn't seek professional counseling until it was way too late and they were over the edge with their compulsive behavior. That's what the therapists had been telling them in psychotherapy group. There was help available, but people had to realize the resources were there before they fell overboard and started looking for a raft.

"Mother, look at all that smoke over there. It looks like something's on fire," Harold said. All three of them, including the driver, looked toward the pitch black smoke.

"No, amigo, there is a gun battle over that hill. Revolutionaries are fighting for their freedom," the driver said. As the truck got closer and closer, they could hear the rapid fire of machine guns and grenade launchers.

"Revolution?" asked Harold. "Do you think it's a good idea for us to continue, driver?"

"Si, señor. Mr. Caesar Manuel is protected from the revolutionary army. You are safe, señor."

The driver continued down the road as the three passengers looked out the windows at truckloads of people on the road, carrying all their personal belongings, leaving their once beautiful country due to the revolution and the chemical poisoning of their land.

"It looks as if they are all fleeing from some kind of terrorism, doesn't it, Mrs. Simmons," said Cynthia.

"Yes, child, and that terrorist is Harry Simmons. Just wait until I see him. We'll only be staying tonight, and then we'll spend the rest of our time at the hotel. I don't think it's too safe for you children out here, with all of this fighting going on."

"I agree with you, Mother. Besides, I don't want anything to happen to you or Cynthia. We'll leave Uncle Harry's place in the morning."

They approached the outskirts of the plantation. It was a beautiful plantation, and the house was magnificent. A sign indicated, "C. Manuel's Tobacco Plantation."

"Why, this looks like Buckingham Palace, with all of the carefully trimmed shrubbery and tropical plants. Isn't it beautiful, honey?" Cynthia said to Harold.

"Yes, and look up, way above on the top of that hill. That must be Uncle Harry's, or Cesar Manuel's, house. It looks like an old Colonial mansion with all of those pillars in front, and it's huge!"

"Yes, child, Harry said he has fourteen separate rooms and three separate guest houses, along with separate quarters for his workers and private entourage right on his 2350-acre farm."

"I thought it was 200 acres, Mother. Did Uncle Harry purchase more property?"

"He sure did. From what I heard, he's trying to buy this whole country, but the government won't permit it," Paula said as she gazed at the beautiful scenery up to the mansion.

"I know I've never seen such a beautiful place," Cynthia remarked. "Hearst Castle, the Hearst Castle in San

Simeon. That's where I used to go when I was in private school as a child, along with all the other little rich kids. This place looks like that, except for the house being architecturally different."

"We're finally here!" exclaimed Harold. "And look, there's Uncle Harry . . . er, I mean, Uncle Caesar Manuel on the patio waiting for us."

Paula and Cynthia looked and saw Mr. Cesar Manuel waiting for them. He was the spitting image of what Harold Junior would look like maybe thirty to forty years down the road.

"Uncle Manuel," Harold said, and they hugged and embraced each other. Paula stayed in the car, looking over her face for a smear in her make-up due to the humidity.

"Uncle Manuel," Harold said, hugging Cynthia, "this is my fianceé, Cynthia Hunter. Cynthia, this is my Uncle Manuel."

"It's a pleasure to meet you. Aren't you a beautiful thing? It looks like Harold has finally established a great deal of class. Why, darling, you could be a model, with your looks," Harry said.

Cynthia blushed, and Paula commenced to get out of the car.

"And look who we have here. It's my loving and talented sister-in-law, the jewel of the whole Simmons family tree. How are you doing, Paula?" Harry said as he embraced her.

But Paula was onto Harry's tricks. He'd always had a way with words and women, and he figured he could charm Paula and get her to have mercy on his dear soul before the fireworks began.

"Mr. Manuel, how are you?" Paula said in a completely businesslike manner.

Harry looked stung and prepared himself for a long lecture. He waited for some of the things that she used to tell him for years, like how he used and abused people for his own self-worth and personal gain.

"Manuel," Paula said, "you have a beautiful farm, and I certainly like the way you have landscaped."

"Why, thank you," he said as he escorted them into the house. Each and every room was exclusively decorated in French Provincial furniture and designed and decorated by a French designer.

"Well, Manuel, I can see that your taste in the good life hasn't changed since you left Las Vegas," Paula said as she walked through the rooms. Not a picture was off-center or a mirror was smeared, or a table had a speck of dust on it.

"Uncle Manuel," Harold said, "this is the type of house Cynthia and I want when we get married. This place is out-of-sight!"

"Yes, Mr. Manuel, this mansion looks like a palace out of a fairy tale," Cynthia said as she admired the furniture and how it coordinated with the style and decor in each room.

"Enough of this formality, Cynthia. From now on, you can call me Uncle Manuel. And when you're in the U.S., Caesar Manuel translates to Harry Simmons. And remember one thing, little darling, Caesar Manuel translates from Spanish to English to mean King of all Men."

"Now I knew he's flipped out," Paula muttered under her breath. Harold and Cynthia looked at Harry, aka Caesar, as if trying to understand where the hell he was coming from.

Harry hadn't changed one bit, Paula thought to herself. As a matter of fact, he'd gotten much worse, and this time he had really gone overboard.

"Cynthia, where are your parents? Did they decide not to come after all?" Harry asked in a voice that evidenced surprise. Harry had done a little research on the Hunter fortune and wanted to talk over some prospective business in the tobacco industry.

"They decided to stay at the hotel in town. They're on a long-awaited second honeymoon, and said they'll see you before they leave," Cynthia said, sticking so close to Harold that it looked like that crazy glue stuff had put them together forever.

"Now, I want you all to make yourselves completely at home. There are tennis courts near the guest house, and the indoor pool is on the left wing of the main house, and the outdoor pool is near the guest house where you two little lovebirds will be staying. Oh, and there is one other thing. When I found out about the little expectant mother, I had my attorney draw up some land-grant deeds. Here are the papers right here." Harry handed the papers to Harold.

"Look at this, Cynthia," Harold said in a state of complete surprise. "Uncle Manuel is giving us over 200 acres of his land and over a quarter of a million dollars to start building a home right here in Venezuela."

Paula had to find a seat; she felt like she was about to faint. She asked the maid to bring her a large shovel because Harry, aka Caesar Manuel, was full of shit. The nerve of him, lying to Harold and Cynthia about what he was going to give them. Why, he never even deeded that house in Las Vegas over to her to distribute the money among the members of the family. What a manipulator!

"Uncle Manuel, we have a bit of bad news pertaining to these grant deeds," Harold Junior said in a low-pitched tone of voice.

Good, Paula thought to herself. Harold is finally

standing up to Harry. He's going to tell him he won't accept the land and will make it on his own.

"You see, Uncle," Harold continued, "Cynthia is expecting twins, so you need to rewrite the deeds."

Oh my God, if that crazy-ass nigger son of mine ain't like his daddy and uncle, the sun won't shine tomorrow. Why, they both are trying to con each other out of what little bit they truly have in life, and that ain't a damn thing.

Paula asked the maid, who was serving cold lemonade, to bring two large shovels because the two of them were full of shit. Cynthia didn't understand what Paula meant, but Harry and Harold did. Now she knew exactly what old Harry was doing. He was up to his old tricks again, trying to turn Harold against her by making all of those promises. Well, this time it wouldn't work. She'd been going through this shit for over thirty years, first with her dead husband before he died, and now with Harold Jr. It was a good thing she'd been in therapy and knew how to turn this whole thing around in her favor.

The nerve of Harry, trying to manipulate Harold and Cynthia with those fake deeds! Common sense should tell them that Americans weren't even permitted to own property in this country. They were only permitted to lease property for a period of a hundred years. Paula used her own therapeutic techniques to see through what Harold Junior and Harry were doing to each other's minds.

"You are all probably exhausted after that long drive, and with all of this humidity that we're having. I'm completely drenched. I'll have Mr. Belli, my butler, show the three of you to your quarters so you can get freshened up."

"Yeah, that sounds like a good idea. Come on, Cynthia, let's go get into something more comfortable," said Harold.

"That sounds like a winner," Cynthia replied, and they both followed Mr. Belli, Harold's new English butler, to their rooms.

"You two go right ahead. Your Uncle Caesar Manuel and I got to discuss a little bit of family business. I'll be right with you," Paula said as the two proceeded through the double French doors and toward the rear of the mansion. They jumped into a four-seat golf cart vehicle.

"Well, Mr. Harry Simmons," Paula said in a tight voice, "you seem to be doing pretty well for yourself. You got this fabulous mansion, you got millions and millions of dollars, and you got slaves working right here on your plantation." Paula placed the emphasis on the word slaves.

"Paula, I don't want to argue with you. I just want you and Harold and Harold's guests to have an nice time while you're visiting me. Make yourself at home, darling, and if there's anything that you want, just ring that little old bell over there, the servant's bell."

"Harry, I want the truth." Paula went over to get the bell. "So, can you hear this little old bell ringing? You're up to something, Harry Simmons, and from the looks of things, this thing that you're doing this time is the grand-daddy of them all. So, do you want to tell me what you're up to, or do I have to ring this little old bell a little louder?"

"What do you mean, Paula? What could I possibly be up to in this neck of the woods? I'm just living off the money that I invested in a good old stock by the name of Parlay. The returns were great," Harry said in a sarcastic tone of voice.

"Harry, who do you think you're talking to? Do I have to ring this bell louder so I can get the truth out of you, or will you be a bigger fool than I thought you were and continue to run guns to both faction groups in this revolution that they're having down here?" Paula said. She started ringing that little servant's bell louder and louder until finally Harry grabbed it, not to stop the ringing of the bell, but to stop Paula from talking so much and steadily figuring his motives out.

"How did this revolution occur, Harry? I noticed that as soon as you moved here, lo and behold, a full-fledged revolution just pops up out of the clear blue sky. Why, these people were living in harmony and then here you come, the so-called King of the Crossroaders. You're no King of the Crossroaders. You're just a fake and a fraud. And now they'll give you a new title: King of the Slaveholders. That's what you are, Harry, King of the Slaveholders. It's the very thing that you've always been against in your entire life, the Big Machine, the Big Corporation, and now you're the ringleader. Are you going to tell me the truth about what's going on," she said, grabbing the bell back, "or will I have to get a little louder with this bell, your so-called servant's bell? Is this the bell that you use, Harry Simmons, to make your slaves jump?" Paula threw the bell down on the marble floor so hard that it cracked and broke.

The servants in the kitchen began to clap their hands and laugh.

"Harry Simmons has just been dethroned as the King of the Slaveholders," Paula yelled out.

"Paula, I thought that you would finally be proud of me and what I've accomplished for the family. But there you go, running off your mouth like you have for the past thirty years, and making nasty accusations that I'm running guns to the people that I love and who love me."

"Love you?" Paula yelled. "They're just trying to get the opportunity to cut your throat, Harry! I saw those people you turned into peasants walking down the road, their heads lowered to the ground in despair, worried from losing every single thing that they owned, just because of your greed, Harry. You've turned into the very thing that your parents used to warn you about staying away from—an exploiter of others for your own personal wealth and self-attainment. Is this part of another parlay, Harry? If it is, I can tell you right now that it won't work, because God don't like evil, and this has to be the most heinous and devilish thing that you have ever done."

"You came all the way from Las Vegas to blame me for this revolution?" Harry shouted. "I had nothing to do with it. It's a political problem within the system, and I'm only trying to protect my own property and self-interest and make a decent living for myself."

"Harry Simmons, when have you ever made a decent living for yourself? Don't forget, I know where you come from, and I know where you're going, unless you stop this game of yours. You're in this revolution too deep already, and unless you get out now, you'll sink without any life preserver. So abandon ship now while you have a chance."

211

19

Harold finished showering and caught a tram back to the main house while Cynthia rested in the guest house. As he walked up to the door in the sitting room, he couldn't help but overhear the heated conversation between his mother and his role model, Uncle Harry.

"You're up to no good, Harry," Paula yelled out. "I can see it in these people's faces how you touched them in some way or another. Your tactics of selling weapons is causing the genocide of this whole once peace-loving people," she shouted.

"What the hell are you talking about, Paula? See what in their faces? Touched them?"

"You're a compulsive power fanatic, Harry."

"What are you pretending to be now, a psychic reader?"

"It's that obsession and that compulsive behavior that's driving you, Harry. You can't leave well enough alone, can you? You had a fortune, and now you're reinvesting that money again, and again and again, until you've parlayed the hell out of your whole life, Harry."

Paula began to cry, and Harold rushed in. "You leave my mother alone, you mother-fucking gangster and crook!" Harold held his mother. "Let me tell you something," Harold continued, "if you ever hurt my mother again, I'll kill your ass. Let's go back to the hotel, Mother. I can see that we're no longer wanted around here."

"No. No, wait," said Harry frantically. "Okay, I'll give up all of this. Just don't leave me. I need help, help in controlling this devil of devious behavior. I need my family back. Don't leave me like those other wives left me, and my children. You're the only family I have left, and I need all of you. I'll retire from the hustling game and get therapy; just don't leave me." Harry began to cry, and Paula and Harold went over and consoled him. "I'll give all of this up if you two will help me get over this compulsive greed and money-taking syndrome. The fault isn't all mine; I'm a victim of circumstances."

"Yeah," Paula said. "Everybody has a different compulsion. Ladies who shop at the mall and max out their credit cards, or the people who can't stop eating. It's a disease that can only be treated with professional therapy. Society is compulsive, and people are only the products of what they hear and see on television and listen to on the radio. That's why people must seek professional help when those problems turn into a habit. You'll find that the money you spend on therapy doesn't amount to one-third the money you'd spend on gambling it away foolishly. You see, Harry, for the past year I've been getting psychotherapy for my compulsive gambling and I've managed to keep my gambling habit at bay."

"That's great, Paula," Harry said, wiping the tears from his face. "Do you think I could get professional help for my habits?"

"Where there's a will, there's a way, Harry. All you have to do is be truthful with yourself, and the rest of the therapy will work out just like clockwork. First you must realize that you do have a problem."

"Mother, I couldn't be more proud of you. I have a confession to make, too. Cynthia and I have been in therapy for the past four months."

"You have?" said Paula as she wiped her eyes with the handkerchief Harry gave her. "It's no wonder you've been doing so well. You've made a dramatic change since a year ago when you were out on that corner in North Las Vegas dealing those drugs. I'm so proud of you." She started crying all over again. "Come to think of it, son, what type of problems are you having? You don't gamble, and you're not a drug user. If you don't mind me asking, what is your problem?"

"Cynthia and I have a problem with excessive sex. All we do is have sex all day and all night . . . in the shower, on the toilet stool, under the kitchen table, in the guest house. All we do is make love all day, and with the babies coming, we had to seek professional help."

"Well, take it from me," Paula said, amazed at his candidness, "when those babies arrive, you and Cynthia will find plenty of other things to do. Those babies got the Simmons blood, and if they're boys or girls, you'll be so busy with them you won't have time for life's little pleasures for a while." Paula and Harry began to laugh so hard at Harold and his acknowledgement of his and Cynthia's problem that they began to cry and hugged each other. They agreed to help one another control their excessive behavior.

Three days passed, and every night Paula could hear the helicopters landing and taking off all throughout the night. She wondered if she should ask Harry about all the noise and what the hell was going on over on the other side of that hill where the butler had told her Mr. Manuel had several warehouses. She hoped Harry was moving all of those weapons elsewhere and would stick to his word. Harry hadn't even talked about his plans, how he was going to sell or lease his plantation to one of the tobacco corporations. Today she would talk to him and find out if he was a man of his word.

At the breakfast table, Paula said, "You know, I had the most unusual dream last night." Harry, Harold and Cynthia were eating. "I had a dream that I was in the military," Paula continued in a low-pitched voice as she remembered. "Yes, and we were on a battlefield where helicopters were coming in and out, night and day, dropping off supplies like machine guns and other deadly weapons. I can't recall who it was, but one of my family members was wounded severely, and I had to call for a helicopter medical evacuation team to come and rescue him or her."

"You know, Mrs. Simmons, I took a class once at Yale in dream interpretation," said Cynthia. The other three listened with eagerness. "The class was called Interpreting Dreams, and we used Sigmund Freud's book on the subject. The dream you had could be interpreted as a conscious rejection of someone not sticking to a previous commitment. Just thinking about it makes you angry and you can just feel something happening to that person, something very tragic. You're trying to avoid that from happening."

"That must be why I keep on having that dream. Anger and disappointment. Yes, it all makes sense now. Thank you, Cynthia." Paula took her hand to show Cynthia how much she appreciated her analysis of the dream that had been haunting her for the past few nights.

"Mother, I've been hearing helicopters all night long myself, and these are large helicopters. One night I woke up, and there were several large army helicopters right over that mountain, landing and taking off all night long," Harold told the group as they sipped on some English tea.

"They're coming from my warehouse," Harry said. He knew damn well that Paula didn't have any dreams. She just wanted information on when he was planning to vacate this living paradise that could turn into a living hellhole unless he took swift and direct action fast. "Those Cobra and Huey helicopters are taking all of the supplies out of the warehouse and placing them in another warehouse outside the city."

"Oh, so you are making plans to move and finally retire?" Paula said.

"Why, yes. I've made all the necessary arrangements, and now all I have to do is have my attorney draft up some legal documents to sign off this whole plantation to the Phillip Morris Corporation," Harry said in confidence.

"You'd better let me see the papers, Harry. You could be signing the whole family fortune away, so let me proofread those documents," Paula said. She kept on insisting that she review the documents before Harry signed them.

"I was once a court clerk, and I used to proofread documents for my father's corporation, Uncle Manuel," Cynthia said. She had built up the courage to call Harry Uncle, but was confused about whether to call him Harry, Caesar, or Manuel. "You better let me take a look at those documents. One time this unscrupulous and fictitious company tried to take my father's whole business just by writing up a bogus legal contract. Let me proofread those documents for you."

"Thank you. Why, if it weren't for you, ladies, I think I'd be homeless and without a pot to pee in. I really appreciate your concern, but my attorney will take care of all the legal formalities."

"You better be careful, Uncle. Just look at what happened to Kareem Abdul Jabbar and Billy Joel. They both trusted their attorneys, and those attorneys took them for over a hundred million dollars. Let me take a look at those papers. After all, I am heir to the Simmons estates."

"Look, I haven't got much time right now. Please excuse me from the table. I have a million things to do today." Harry threw his napkin on the table and left in a panic.

Paula called out, "Oh, Mr. Manuel, you left your hat. I'll bring it to you." When she caught up to him, she asked him to step into the sitting room, the same room where their first argument and agreement occurred. She closed the door behind them.

"You promised us, Harry Simmons. We made a family agreement that you would stop all that gun running and get the hell out of this place as soon as you could. Now you're up to your old tricks again, buying more weapons and supplying those armies and revolutionary guerrillas with arms," Paula said, very disappointed.

"No, Paula, I'm taking inventory of all the weapons that I have stockpiled and I'm selling those weapons back to the company that I purchased them from. That's all I'm doing," Harry said in a reasonable tone.

"This time I'm going to believe you, and hope that you have enough sense to get out while you're ahead. You must have over five hundred million dollars or they wouldn't have put you in the *Fortune 500* magazine. What more do you want, Mr. Manuel, King of the Crossroaders and gun runners?"

"Everything has been taken care of, Paula. Just trust me," Harry said as he held Paula's hand and gave her that sad and disparaging look that no one could ever ignore. They opened the door, only to find Harold and Cynthia eavesdropping on their conversation.

"Oh, Mother, I was just going to tell you that Cynthia and I are going into town to do a little shopping. Would you like to join us?" Harold said.

"No, Harold, I think it's time we all leave. I have to get

back and find out how your sister Sylvia is doing. I haven't heard a word from that girl. It's time we were all going back home," she said in a low, tired voice that indicated she had given up on her brother-in-law. Harry had a death wish, and that would be the only thing that could get him out of the hustling game, the game that once you're in it, you're in it for life.

*   *   *

That was the last time she saw or heard from Harry, the King of the Crossroaders, and his newly-won title of King of the Slaveholders. He had turned into a tyrant and a thief, hoarding what little the people had and taking away their culture and rights to exist.

They arrived back in the United States and spent a week with the Hunters in Connecticut, arranging for Harold and Cynthia's wedding, and then Paula took a commercial plane back to Las Vegas. It brought back plenty of memories of that day over fifteen years ago when she'd arrived there with two small children, Harold Junior in her arm and Sylvia in a stroller.

As she reminisced, she could visualize herself getting off that Greyhound bus in downtown Las Vegas, looking at the lights flashing on and off and listening to those slot machines as she carried those two children.

"Yes, girl," Paula said to Barbara, Harold's old girl-friend and the mother of one of Harold's children, "that's the way it was then and that's the way it will always be here in North Las Vegas and the whole world."

"What happened to the home on Alta, and Sylvia?" Barbara asked.

"Well, child, Sylvia finally got her act together and was married to Thomas. They both moved to Atlanta, along with my little granddaughter, and Thomas attended McHarry Medical School. Thomas was a bright young man and his parents were both physicians, so he didn't have any problems completing his medical degree. He was deeply in love with Sylvia and just adored that baby," Paula said with a breath of relief.

"But that beautiful home on Alta, what happened to it, Mrs. Simmons?" Barbara knew that the older woman was tired and disappointed about moving back into the housing project in North Las Vegas after having the time of her life.

"Harry, my so-called brother-in-law, lost the house and everything that went along with it."

"How, Mrs. Simmons?"

"Well, after we left Venezuela where Harry was running guns and spraying those pesticides on the crops and the people, all we heard was that they turned against old Harry and all of the organizations that were paying old Harry off to keep the war going. Some organizations were sending in relief packages of food and medical supplies, but the people never got them because of Harry's black-marketing schemes. They all got clever and staged a coup de grace on him. You see, Harry said he was getting out after just this one more last sting. But it never happened that way. He got further and further and deeper and deeper into that parlay ego trip, and he kept using his investments to get more and more money and notoriety.

"The people, every last one of those organizations, set old Harry up. The Central Intelligence Agency knew that the White House, under the new Clinton Administration, was on to their imperialistic tactics, so the CIA decided Harry would be the fall guy. He had to be eliminated before he went before the Senate Committee on Arms. The FBI wanted Harry back in the States to face charges on robbery and money laundering, and they got with the CIA and the Venezuelan government and tried to devise a plan to get Harry back here to face charges.

"But old Harry was too smart for that bunch. He'd videotaped every last meeting with the heads of governments on his plantation and had recorded every last payoff on videotape. Harry put the fear in them, and they couldn't touch him. So the CIA, FBI and Venezuelan government teamed up with the IRS and confiscated every single thing Harry owned, even the house that was in my name on Alta, just to get Harry to step his black ass back into the United States so they could nab him.

"But that didn't work. All those organizations couldn't touch old Harry, so the United Nations proclaimed that he was harming the environment by spraying those pesticides and destroying the environment by selling all the timber he owned on his property. They sent a delegation to try to talk to him, but he wouldn't see them, so they joined the others and planned a hit on Harry.

"Two of those huge, noisy helicopters just happened to crash while Harry was taking inventory one night in his warehouse where he had all those explosives and ammunition. That fabulous and beautifully decorated mansion all went up in smoke from those explosives. Harry's body was never found, and no one has said a word about the whole incident since then. If Harry wouldn't have lied to me, I would have found out the truth. But I'm so tired of the Simmons' and the games they played. I needed my rest, girl, after thirty years of dealing with a family of con artists. I gave up on trying to help that family.

"Now I'm back here, back in North Las Vegas, in the housing projects where I started. At least I'm accepted just because I'm me, and not because I still have a bankroll, girl, and not because I still know some of the most influential people in the world. I'm back here because this is where I want to be. I may eventually move back to Atlanta, but until then I'm comfortable right here, dealing with those gangs, the drug dealing and the cockroaches all at the same time. And every single night I'm home, I'm comfortable here.

"You see, child, although I had the time of my life with the money and the gorgeous houses and cars, I didn't let that ruin me like the time when I first moved here to Las Vegas, getting instant gratification of winning for the first time on that slot machine. It was a peak experience that ran through my very soul, child, and back then I couldn't stop my compulsive gambling after winning it big for the first time.

"My daughter, Sylvia, had the same instant gratification, smoking those drugs, girl, and Harry had his peak experience when he pulled off Operation Parlay. But Harry just couldn't stop his excessiveness. Luckily I got Sylvia into some therapy before it was too late.

"You know, those drugs and compulsive gambling are both centered in the same pleasure centers of the brain. Yeah, that's what I learned from going to therapy. And that's the reason why some people can't quit their excessive and compulsive behavior. So you see, Barbara, that's why I keep telling you that that's the way it is, and that's the way it always will be with some people."